ALL ANGELS BUT ONE

Zorina Alliata

All Angels but One

Copyright © 2010 Zorina Alliata

Publisher: Better Karma Publishing

www.BetterKarmaPublishing.com

Cover by EOS Grafx

www.eosgrafx.com

ISBN 978-0-9824329-7-6

For the child that I lost and for the child God helped me find

The Lord said, "Go out. Stand on the mountain in front of me. I am going to pass by." As the Lord approached, a very powerful wind tore the mountains apart. It broke up the rocks. But the Lord wasn't in the wind. After the wind there was an earthquake. But the Lord wasn't in the earthquake. After the earthquake a fire came. But the Lord wasn't in the fire. And after the fire there was only a gentle whisper. When Elijah heard it, he pulled his coat over his face. He went out and stood at the entrance to the cave. Then a voice said to him, "Elijah, what are you doing here?"
(1 Kings 19:11-13)

1

New York City, New York
Sunday Night

He was a tall, wiry black man and anyone could see that he had been touched. He walked in his expensive sneakers, but they were only remnants of his life from before. His posture was humble and his eyes kind. He was shaking slightly as he stepped into the church to the crowd's gasps and cheers.

"It's him," the woman next to Grace whispered, overwhelmed. "It's him," and she grabbed Grace's arm and squeezed. Grace shook her off and moved ahead through the crowd. She was too far, still, for a good look.

By the time she reached the main aisle, he had passed through already and was now talking with the minister near the circular altar. She watched as they hugged and shed tears. Then the minister turned around and announced, for the millionth time in the history of the human race, and so loudly she almost covered her ears:

"God loves us! "

The crowd cheered wildly, prayers erupting here, there and everywhere.

"What more proof do we want that God exists?" he continued, his forehead sweating from all the excitement and happiness. "He again talks with us. He chose one of us and blessed us all through him, right here in the Bowery. He touched our souls with His message. Everything will be all right, He said. Everything will be all right."

He paused, tears flowing down his cheeks. "Do you understand?" he asked, walking closer to the front of the crowd, arms opened wide. "Everything will be all right."

Grace fought back tears of her own. Through all the pain, she could still easily recognize the Truth when she heard it. She had no doubt that the tall man had heard some kind of message from God, even though the way he registered it was probably distorted and wishful; but she could almost taste and smell traces of God's soft whisper even from that distance. It felt so good to her, like an embrace she had longed for. Like home.

They were all gathered in the round, in the open space. Usually music was heard during the service, but tonight there was none. The atmosphere was different; the attendees were different. There were no gimmicks and props this time. The emotions ran high and everyone there was absolutely dead serious.

"Let my prayer be set forth in your sight as incense, the lifting up of my hands as the evening sacrifice." Father Williams started. "Grace to you and peace from God our Father and from the Lord Jesus Christ. Worship the Lord in the beauty of His holiness; let the whole earth tremble before him."

People settled down and quietly bowed their heads.

"Everything," enunciated Father Williams. "What does it mean, everything? It is no more or less than every ounce of our being. Our heart, our soul, and our mind. That is what everything means to us. How we are. How we love with our hearts; our essence; our reason. Is God in there? Is God in your soul, in your heart, in your mind? Then you will be all right, because that's the message God gave us through this man."

He moved around the altar, so close to the crowd that they could touch him if they merely raised their arms.

"My faith is practical; I help as I can, with my own two hands. I am not one to easily trust others," he confessed. "I am working on that every day. But because of it, I am also not easily fooled. St. Mark's is no fool's church either. We've been here since New York City became New York City and we've seen it all. But I do believe, friends, that this man has truly heard God. I do not doubt it. The change in him is too drastic. His mind opened, and his soul opened to receive His word. I have never seen anything like it. I am very happy, friends, I am very happy."

He wept a bit again. "I feel validated," he said. "Don't you? All my life I ended my sermons asking you to dare to believe, against the odds sometimes, that God is here and that I am speaking the Truth to you. But now we know. We don't assume, or guess, or hope anymore. Now we know. God is here. And he is asking everything of you. He needs your heart, your soul, and your mind. And then you will be all right."

It had been a short, but effective sermon. They were all sharing a great feeling, a strange feeling that seemed just a bit wrong, like too much honey poured in the tea, too much happiness in one spoon. Some people cried, others smiled. It felt surreal, magical, and slightly frightful.

Grace waited until it was all over. The crowd dispersed long after midnight, emotion pouring out in silent waves throughout the church. The tall man stayed longer, whispering to everyone who came to him. He tirelessly shook their hands and crossed himself and the air in front of him .

Grace left the church with a group of older women, her face half-hidden under her hood. She was tiny and she had mastered the art of sneaking around unobserved; she wore a foundation that made her look pale and common, no lipstick, no eyeliner. Her hair, dyed brown just hours before, was tied up in a sloppy ponytail. Contact lenses to make her blue eyes look brown. No nail polish; no IDs; old, baggy jeans and a black-and-grey hooded sweatshirt.

Once they passed the Aspiration statue, she remained behind the group and waited near the 10th Street exit. It was quiet, if you listened carefully enough; the pavement exuded a warm and peaceful vibe. It was all there, Grace thought. So simple to understand, and yet people were running around, blind and hurried, hitting their heads from rock to rock.

Finally, the tall man came out as well. She didn't expect him to be alone; two friends tagged along. The one on the right was a large black man, with sharp eyes under the visor of his cap. The one on the left was new to the friendship, she thought, watching him shyly trying to keep up the pace. They started to walk down Avenue A, and Grace followed from a distance, carefully rushing from shade to shade. She had mapped the surroundings of the church down to the lower end of Manhattan.

The three men turned on 6th Street and then a small side street, and stopped in front of a brownstone. No one else was around, Grace knew. She checked her watch - it was almost 2:00 AM. The tall man hugged his friends and said goodbye- that's where his apartment was, she knew. As his friends walked away along the dark side street, Grace watched the tall man looking for his keys.

She walked up to him, hood down, eyes wide open.

"Hi", she said, and she saw she startled him. "I… I followed you from the church."

He relaxed, smiled. Like just being in a church ever guarantees anything.

"Hi", he said, and his voice was so soft, so good.

"Can we talk?" she said. "I really need your help."

"Uh... okay," he agreed. He *was* good, all good inside now, like sweet bread rising in a warm oven. Almost disgustingly good, Grace thought.

"Damn landlord," he mumbled. "This lock never works right."

He pulled out a credit card and jammed the lock until it gave in. He stepped into the dimly-lit hallway and Grace followed closely.

"Hey," she whispered, and he turned towards her. They were almost touching.

She took out her gun and shot him between the eyes, with rehearsed precision. She held onto him as he was thrown backwards, a surprised look in his eyes that immediately gave out to a blank expression. She rushed to catch him as he fell down, her fingers dipping into the bloody back of his skull, and when he breathed out his last breath she kissed him and inhaled it all, hers to keep forever. Tears of joy came out of her eyes when the taste of Heaven touched her soul.

■■ ∎

"Detective Walker," he introduced himself to the sergeant. He was a tall man in his 50s, with wild curly hair. He seemed tired and his blue eyes were squinting. The morning light was still weak. "Whacha got?"

"Shooting," said the sergeant and spit out his gum. "'Bout the fourth one this week in this neighborhood."

"Huh," said Walker. They walked together toward the body and the detective got his notebook out. "Gangs?" he asked.

"Probably," said the sergeant. "I don't know what the hell they have to fight about all the time. Morons, all of them."

They went inside, where several policemen were rushing about. Flash cameras were going off every few seconds. The victim lay close to the elevator area. The light was dim - Walker looked up and saw that only one lonely light bulb was hanging from the ceiling.

He stepped closer. The victim was a black male in his thirties, he wrote down. He had been shot in the forehead, right between the eyes. There was blood on the wall behind him. Part of his skull had been blown away in the back of the head.

"Hey, Doc," he saluted the coroner. "What's up?"

"Gun shot. A 38 special. Probably had a silencer since no one heard it. I'd have to get back to you, but the position doesn't make sense."

"What do you mean? He was killed somewhere else and dragged here?"

"No, no," the doctor protested. He looked tired too. "Look at the blood splat on that wall. He was killed here. The thing is, by the look of the wound, he was shot from very close. Yet he didn't fly back almost at all. If he was shot at the door, he should have been thrown all the way into the wall."

"Hmm. What the heck does that mean?"

"Not sure right now. Maybe there was a fight. I'll talk to you later. I think I'm done here." The coroner signaled two policemen and they started to prepare a body bag.

Walker returned to the entrance where the sergeant was waiting for him.

"This one of those buildings with a dumb waiter?" he asked, almost smiling, looking at the small box near the elevator. "Long ago, people used to come down from the roof in one of those, and wait inside a building to attack. I got a couple of 'em, yeah. Good times. Ya know, the real New York."

"Doesn't seem to have been used in a long time," the young sergeant shrugged. "The door lock was forced open, probably by jamming something into it.   Guess that's how the killer got in."

"Hmmm. Any witnesses?"

"No, no one," the sergeant said, glancing toward the thick crowd behind the police line. "I have the landlord, he's the one that called the police."

"OK."

The sergeant waved to someone in the hallway and an old, thin man came forward, fidgeting.

"Yeah," he started before Walker had a chance to open his mouth. "Yeah, I found him, right at my door, right there when I opened the door. You know? Was going out, was trying to... to get coffee, and there he was. Yeah. So I called 911. Yeah."

He looked bad, his face yellow and long, his eyes bouncing in all directions.

"Coffee, really?" Walker asked, not expecting an answer. The man was going out at five in the morning for a fix, he was sure. He looked around the entrance. "The lock is busted," he said. "Was it like that?"

"No, no, the lock was fine, of course. I guess the killer broke it. Yeah."

"So, Mr..." Walker said.

"Billy, Billy Daves," the landlord offered quickly.

"Mr. Daves. You don't come out looking too good here. The lock is crappy. There is almost no light here. It's like you're inviting trouble. I think we need to report these violations, you know."

"Please," the landlord fidgeted. "This ain't the Plaza, you know. I do what I can, okay? What do you want? He paid his rent on time, you know. He ain't no trouble. He had people in and out all the time, of all kinds. Coulda been anyone."

"Anyone stood out from the crowd?" asked Walker. "They all look like church-goers?"

The landlord lowered his voice. "Some of his old buddies came over almost every day in the last couple of weeks. None looked happy to be here. They also ain't stepped in a church since their mama stopped breastfeedin' 'em."

"Did he owe them money or such?" Walker lowered his voice too.

"I don't know. They don't talk much, those types, and I ain't starting any conversations."

"Do you have their names?"

"Now don't get me in trouble, man," the landlord wailed. "Just ask on the street, okay. Everybody knows who the big guns are."

That was good enough for now, Walker decided. All the landlord wanted was the police out so he could get his fix.

"OK," he said. "You can go. We'll find ya if we have any questions later."

The landlord disappeared quickly out the main door, relieved.

"OK then," said Walker. He took out his cell phone and dialed his boss. "Pete, it's Sieg. What the hell did you send me here for? It's a regular shooting, they had four this week on this very street. No, no, you listen. Why didn't you send Barry, huh? I was comfortable on my couch sleeping there in my boxers, and you make me come here at six in the AM for what?"

He listened for a while as the sergeant waited.

"You've got to be kidding me," he said finally and hung up. "You're not going to believe this," he said to the sergeant, "but this guy apparently talked with God a couple of months ago. Now the Archdiocese is calling and wants the killer on a platter."

They both chuckled. "I am telling you," Walker said, "New York City's got the most crazies per square mile. Let's go up to his apartment."

"Oh, God," somebody cried behind them, "oh, God."

They turned around and were face to face with a minister. He was older, and his forehead was sweaty.

Walker and the sergeant caught him by his arms, as he approached the body.

"Sir," said Walker, "Sir, I am detective Walker. Did you know the victim?"

"I am Father Williams, from St. Mark's," said the priest. "Yes, yes, I know him, I know him well. He was at the church last night. What happened? What happened to him?"

"He was shot in the head at close range," the sergeant answered very matter-of-fact. . "No one saw anything. His two friends left him in front of his house about 2:00 AM last night. Looks like it happened right after."

"But it doesn't make any sense," said the priest. "He was like a local hero, you know. He experienced a miracle. . I mean, even the Archdiocese of New York was investigating and they had reason to believe it was true. But everyone loved him, everyone. People came from everywhere to see him last night, thousands of them. Why would anyone want to kill him?"

"Well," said the sergeant, and handed Walker a sheet of paper. "Volt Jackson, the name. Arrested several times for gang and drug-related activities. Last out of prison five months ago. Three kids with three different women, and never married."

"Hmm," said Walker. "Looks like our picture and your picture, Father, differ quite a bit. Are you sure this is the same guy, your local hero?"

"He's changed," Father Williams said dismissively. "He *was* all that, but not anymore. Believe me, I knew him well. We talked a lot in the last few weeks. He was a changed man, a good man."

Walker and the sergeant exchanged a look.

"Uh-uh," said Walker. "Well. I need to go over there and do my work. Can I reach you at the church then, Father, if I have any other questions?"

"Sure, sure," said the minister.

As Walker turned to leave, the priest grabbed his arm. He sighed. "Yes?"

"I can tell you don't believe," Father Williams said bluntly . "But I don't care if you're not one of the chosen ones. Just do your job, okay? Don't let this miracle make the killer any different than all other killers. Catch him, okay?"

"Will do my best, Father," Walker said and hurried away. Freaks, he murmured. Goddamn freaks, on such a beautiful Monday morning in Manhattan.

2

The Internet got the news by early morning. It rumbled and grumbled and propagated it immediately, with a great buzz. The Internet knew who Volt was; it knew all about his former and current life. It knew the name of his kids and ex-girlfriends, his favorite singer, and his favorite church. It knew his credit card number and what he purchased from where. It knew his real friends and his fake friends, and all that information bubbled up and was shared one more time between people on social networks and TV sites, in repeated links and old videos and interviews. Memorial pages were created by 9:00 AM, and the predominant picture was of Volt's face with a large, sincere smile in one of the rare happy moments of his life, although no one knew what exactly the moment was about.

The Internet soon streamlined the story by aggregating everyone's comments with precision and speed. It was an abominable murder, the Internet decided. It was done by someone who hated God. It was done by someone who is evil.

Matt Reed posted late in the morning, and the Internet watched carefully for his reaction. He and Volt were not buddies, the Internet knew well. Matt did not have any buddies; he was always too tough, too faithful, too damn perfect with his appropriate and meaningful daily quotes from the Bible. He was above most average people, and the Internet respected and feared him because of it. The Internet had felt Matt's condescendence and superiority towards Volt many times over, and did not expect much sympathy. But it expected class and human concern, and that's exactly what Matt Reed gave when he dutifully uploaded the same smiling photo of Volt and a short but poignant obituary. It was nothing like his usual rambling, fierce posts. But the Internet accepted it and moved forward, generating murder theories and coming up with possible suspects, totally missing the point that Matt was politely trying to make when he subtly suggested the murderer was someone from Volt's troubled past and had no link to the extraordinary events in June.

And then the Internet waited on the fifty-seven group, or what was left of it, to speak. There were the sensitive ones, mostly middle-aged or older women, with their boring lives and at least one cat each. They blogged daily. They "connected", their favorite word, and "reached" to others, trying to "help everyone all the time. They were preachy and swore that every little thing that happened to them was a miracle: meeting an old friend, finding a long-lost book, saving a wounded bird the cat had dragged in. They thought everyone was like them, because they were so full of themselves they never really tried to understand others. They were sure lots of people needed saving; or were sick in some way; or had been left and cheated by loved ones. They thought Volt's murderer was a very lonely and desperate man who just needed someone to listen.

At the other extreme, there were the scientific ones. They thought nothing was a miracle. They tried to explain the events in June as a government experiment, an alien visit, a meteorological anomaly, a moon flare, a sun flare, an asteroid, a Russian conspiracy and a Chinese conspiracy. Sometimes, their sadness would penetrate through their dry explanations. What if? One of them would ask once in a while. Others fought to find links between science and God by discussing the golden ratio, the divine proportion, even the philosophy of pi. Tried to put Him into equations and formulas and patterns. Poured through old documents and secret church rituals, to find hidden clues. They thought Volt's murder was drug-related as had been his life before.

Then there were the true believers. They were not very surprised that God had paid them a visit back in June.

They had been expecting it, almost. They were the ones who thought their lives had been predetermined and pre-planned before their souls were even born into bodies. They lived in the moment and were content within the moment. They had no big ambitions. June's event was a validation for them, and it had caused no emotional upheaval. They thought Volt died simply because his time on Earth had come to an end.

The rest were all over the map; from the fanatics to the depressed, all colors of the spectrum were represented. Opinions varied, but overall they thought the murder was related to the June events.

The Internet knew that all of the fifty-seven were struggling, with a different intensity and at different levels. Some were struggling because they saw God; but most struggled because God came and then he left them again, alone, in the dark of that June night, with nothing to hold on to.

3

Bethesda, Maryland
Monday

It was 7 in the evening and the darkness was already blanketing the area.. The limo pulled slowly up to the front of the gate, and waited. The driver stepped out when the blonde, slim woman appeared. He courteously held the door for her. She climbed in. nd then they were gone.

Grace climbed the side fence easily. The alarm had been disabled that morning, she had seen the truck and the guy coming in, tapping his working hat. Her body felt sore all over. She had taken the $20 Chinese bus from New York to DC, then had come straight to the house. She had been standing behind the line of old oaks all day, with only two bottles of water and a bag of chips.

It had been a busy day. The house had had several visitors, and, not much to her surprise, O'Dell had shown up as well. Grace backed up a few more steps, even though she was far away enough. He stayed about an hour.

Then, the husband and two daughters left, along with several large bags, in an SUV. The husband did not look happy. The girls, one blonde, one brunette, kept arguing. They had expensive outfits and the oldest, not more than 11 years old, wore diamond earrings. The husband was nonchalant in his Armani suit, keys from the Mercedes dangling in his impatient hand. There was no waving good-bye from the house.

Around lunch time, the charity trucks started to arrive. They loaded furniture, lamps, paintings and ottomans. The blonde lady came out of the house for the first time to supervise. She wore white pants, high heels and a baby blue shirt. Her hair revealed some black roots, but it still looked great pulled in a tight ponytail. She had green eyes and her arms looked like she was working out a lot. As soon as Grace caught a glimpse of her face, she knew it was true. She had really been touched.

Grace crossed the perfect lawn and took out the tension wrench from her backpack. The lock on the back door was easy to pick, and she did it in less than a minute. There was no one around, she could tell. No people, no pets, no ghosts. She walked into the large kitchen and then into the entrance hall. It was a huge house and her steps resonated on the marble floor. Lots of furniture was gone, and the walls were empty.

As she found her way into the living room in the dim light, she bumped into an armchair. She let out a moan; she had stubbed her big toe. A couch, TV and a chair were left in the living room. Grace sat down, tired, her right foot pulsating with pain.

It was almost midnight when the humming noise of the limo pulling up front woke her up. She got the syringe out of her backpack and hid behind the door. Soon, the blonde woman stepped in and, as she closed the door behind her, was face to face with Grace. Before the blonde could say anything, Grace grabbed her arm and stuck the needle in, and let everything go under the skin, into the blood.

"What... what... what?" the blonde woman gasped.

"It's okay," said Grace. "It's okay. Just sit down."

She helped the woman to the armchair in the living room.

"Who are you?" the woman asked.

"I'm your guardian angel," said Grace, hoping to keep her quiet. "You're Dinah Sherry, married, two kids, main preoccupation your appearance and your social calendar."

"Guardian angel?" said the woman, and her eyes vacillated between joy and skepticism. "But then what did you shoot into my arm?"

"Poison," Grace said. "It's okay. Your time has come, that's all. Didn't you have a divine experience recently?"

"Yes, yes, I did," said Dinah, her eyes now showing her fear. "Poison?"

"It's okay, you will die tonight," Grace said matter-of-fact. "Don't worry, okay? You're going to Heaven. He doesn't touch people for no reason. He always has a reason. You'll just go a bit earlier than planned, that's all."

"But... my babies," the woman said. "They're so young."

"They'll be okay," Grace lied. The kids were rotten already, she could see it in the way their fingertips and lips moved.

The woman didn't say anything more. She was trying to figure it out in her head; she was a smart one, Grace could tell. Did fine before, when she married rich. Never let her guard down. Except in the last few months, after God had talked with her and turned everything upside down.

Grace looked at her watch. There were still about 15 minutes left before Dinah would be ready for the next shot.

"Why don't you tell me about when God spoke to you?" she asked.

Dinah sighed. She was trying to move but her muscles were stiff. "What kind of poison?" she asked, her voice weakened.

"Home-made," said Grace. "Won't be long now. Don't worry, you'll love it in Heaven. Here the whole world is made of nothing but empty rock. But there you will be free, and right."

"I went to Catholic school when I was a little girl, you know," the woman said, trying to smile. "My Dad made me. Said I was wild, too smart for my own good, but so was he. And so is my little girl. Stupid people call it crazy or wild, but I call it highly intelligent."

Grace didn't say anything. There was a streak of madness in the woman's blood: she could see its path clearly from generation to generation. High intelligence had helped her integrate into society and pretend to be normal. Her little girl would not be so lucky.

"I never believed in God, though," the woman said. "I believed in me alone and making my own luck. And it was all going according to plan, under control, you know, for a while. My little girl got into the best private school. My oldest plays soccer with all the daughters of all important diplomats in DC. Our best friends are doctors, lawyers and CEOs. We party every weekend with the elite of DC. We were present at all important events. Such a lovely couple, they said. They envied us. They all envied us. But there were problems no one knew about, just under the surface. I think my husband is having an affair, traveling *all* the time, and it's like you could tell he just didn't want to be here. And when he is home, he only drinks all the time. My little one was almost kicked out of school, and was out of control at home, and I can see in her eyes that she hates me, and I don't know why because I love her more than life itself. My oldest has nothing but Cs in all classes."

Grace nodded her head, pretending to understand. There were still about 10 minutes left.

"Tell me about when God spoke to you," she said again, and she sounded almost like she was pleading. She missed it so much, she could feel her body trembling in waiting.

"Well, I was at this charity event in Manhattan, you know," Dinah said. "The annual ball they have for the highest contributors."

"Oh, so you gave a lot to charity?" asked Grace.

"Um, not really, not any more than needed for, you know, some tax relief. But we were friends with the CEO of the nonprofit and he invited us to sit at his table. So anyway, I suddenly felt kind of sick. Maybe it was the shrimp, who knows. Just not feeling great, you know. I excused myself and went to the bathroom, and that's where is happened."

Grace chuckled. It was just like Him, with the sense of humor.

"I was washing my face, and when I looked up, there was no mirror. It was... I could see the whole Universe. It's hard to explain, there are no words, you know?"

Grace nodded. She knew.

"And then I think He walked by, just ever so gently, and I just felt the air around me warm up. It smelled of flowers and mint and... and honey, maybe. Of everything I always wanted but didn't know. I think I saw his footprint, bathed in light, for a split second before it disintegrated into even more light. I saw how I was wrong, I understood everything at once, and I heard him breath, and then I heard Him talk. 'Come back to me,' He said. And I wanted to, so badly. And I did."

Grace was so moved she took Dinah's hand in her own. "You are so blessed," she said. "You don't even know how blessed you are. Even angels rarely hear Him speak."

Dinah had tears in her eyes. Her face was pale and sweaty, and her hands had frozen in the middle of a convulsed move.

"So why then did He send an angel to kill me?" she managed to whisper faintly .

Grace laughed sadly. "He didn't send me. "

It was about time, and Grace moved on the armchair, taking the woman in her arms, and gave her the second shot. Dinah breathed harder and harder, and her eyes clung to Grace's eyes, silently imploring. And then it finally came, her last breath, and Grace kissed her on the lips and took it all inside, her whole life story, her pain and moments of happiness and love for her kids, her encounter with God, and along with it a small piece of divinity came rushing into her lungs.

■■ ■ ■

"Any news?" asked the Captain, and handed Walker a large mug of coffee.

"I suppose you mean about the divine intervention case," said Walker, slurping. "Let me guess, phone's ringing off the hook 'cause all the religious nuts in the tri-state area are calling."

"Kinda," the Captain chuckled. "So, where are we?"

"Well, the analysis so far says our shooter is a very short man – maybe five-four, if even. He's also familiar with the surroundings because many buildings around have permanent unofficial guards outside and some have cameras in the street. But the killer was not seen by any. We have no visuals at all. Was tryin' to talk with some of the informants to see if they heard or saw anything."

"Hmm," muttered the Captain. "If it was someone from the 'hood, it will come up sooner or later. A short guy, you say?"

"There's also weird stuff," Walker said. "The killer held the victim as he shot him, apparently. We found some fibers, but nothing special, from a common sweatshirt or something similar. We found a fragment of a hair, or so we thought. Turns out they couldn't get any DNA out of it. It was more like some kind of artificial hair. But it was dyed brown. The guys at the lab were very confused about it, I'm sure it will be all spelled out in their report."

"It's just weird until we find the explanation," the Captain dismissed it. "We'll keep at it, as you says. We'll sift through the neighborhood a bit more."

"I talked with some of his old buddies. Landlord said they stopped by often in the last couple of weeks, and did not look happy. There's the three of them who run the neighborhood. Jackson used to be with them but then he turned into a church staple and forgot them. Apparently they were trying to convince him to get back to his old ways. Jackson had some good connections that got lost when he started believin'. But all three have strong alibis for last night."

"Check and check again," said the Captain. "Alibis could be fake, I would expect it in this case."

"We did," Walker sighed. "It all verifies. They were at a club in Manhattan. They're on the video and everything."

"What about the apartment? Was there any sign of break up, or a fight?"

"I don't think the killer went to the apartment. The door was locked. Everything was in order, although he didn't have much. Sparse furnishings, some Chinese food, and a bed without a mattress. Landlord said he gave away lots of his old stuff to charity lately."

"Hmm. That's unusual, I'd say."

"Well, something to keep in mind, for sure," Walker sighed. "Unfortunately our victim made a few thousand new friends recently. A strong possibility is one of your good Christians doing it."

"That minister says there's no way," said the Captain. "He can't fathom a reason why a believer would do that."

"Sure," punctuated Walker loudly, "since Christians have behaved so gingerly throughout the history of human race. None of them ever harmed another, right?"

The Captain shrugged and got up for another cup of coffee. "Look, this was a big deal at the church there. These guys took it seriously. The Archdiocese had assigned a priest to look into it, and so far had no doubts that it happened."

"I know," sighed Walker. "I tell you what. I will not exclude or include anyone based on their faith alone. I will go about it as I went about all other hundreds of cases I had. I talked with my informants, and I talked with the minister. I have no leads as of yet, but something will come up. It always does. You know that as well as I do."

The Captain nodded his head in agreement. "The Archdiocese investigator wants to talk with you," he said. "His name is Father O'Dell. He called me late last night.

He says maybe he can help put together a profile of the killer."

"Sure, I'll take it," said Walker. "Whatever helps."

The Captain finished his coffee with a big gulp and put his arms on the desk.

"So what's your theory? Unofficially?" he asked, leaning forward.

"Crazy religious asshole who either envied Jackson, or adored him so much he wanted him to go to Heaven early," Walker answered in a single breath. "Something along those lines."

"Hmm," muttered the Captain. "Well, let's keep at it. Who knows where the cameras are on that street? What kind of religious motive could someone have to kill Jackson? And, any short assholes who live around there? Or women who hated him? What about the gun, any leads on that? As you says, something will turn up from somewhere."

His phone started ringing, so Walker tapped his fingers to his temple in a brief salute and got up to leave. He didn't even make it to the door before the Captain called him back. He had hung up the phone, eyes sparkling.

"This might confirm your theory, Sieg," he said. "There's been another murder in DC. A woman who says she talked with God a couple of months ago. Go there, see what you can find. O'Dell called; he's already there and he will wait for you. I will make sure you get all the help from our colleagues there, too."

4

Elizabeth, New Jersey
Tuesday

Grace checked into the Days Inn right off the Turnpike.
She had taken the Greyhound early in the morning and
was tired. She needed to shower and change, and eat
something warm. There wasn't much time left. It was
almost noon already.

The foot was still hurting; the toenail was now completely
black and the toe was red and swollen. She washed it in
cold water and kept it up for a while.

Two hours later, feeling stronger, she checked out and
took a cab to a side street off Rahway Avenue, and
walked from there. It was nice outside and the streets
and houses seemed so small after the day spent in
Bethesda looking at all the mansions. Grace was limping
only a little, so she picked up the pace.

The house was painted white and blue, with a small
porch in the front. She knocked at the door, her
backpack hanging on one shoulder only. She waited a
minute, checking her fingernails, and then knocked
again.

A man in a wheelchair opened the door. "Yes?" he asked with a heavy accent.

He was in his fifties, slim, with thinning brown hair. He had a common face but his bright eyes spelled insight and intelligence.

"Hi," Grace said in a cheery voice. "I am from the Archdiocese of New York. I am here to talk with you about your recent experience."

"Can I see some ID?" the man asked dryly.

"Sure!" she chirped. She pulled out her ID card and showed it to him. Usually these people had their guard down; they went through a phase where they thought everything was beautiful and other people were good. They disarmed their houses and left their doors opened, and trusted and believed anyone who talked with them. Obviously it was not the case with this guy.

"OK," he said, still reserved. "Well, come on in then."

He maneuvered his wheelchair through the narrow hallway and into the living room; she followed. He

chance. It's just I always end up working with a bunch of idiots."

"Uh-uh," she approved. Whatever he was touched with, it surely did not make him humble.

"So I was driving home at night, thinking of work, you see. And I noticed there was no one on the highway. It was eerie, you see. No other cars behind me or in front of me, or on the opposite lanes. I was thinking that was weird, and then the big light came. It was like a big truck suddenly opened his lights on me. And the car kind of stopped but I was still driving, somehow."

He paused, trying to find words.

"I understand," she nodded. "It usually is very hard to explain. Just tell me in your own words, it's okay."

"It was Him, it was God, I know it. I felt it inside me. It was like E.T., you know, these little lights turned on inside of me, like I reached the mother ship. And I wasn't even a believer until then, I just resisted Him and now I don't know why. It all made sense."

"Did you hear Him talk?" asked Grace.

"I'm not sure," he said. "It was higher than my senses, somehow. I didn't hear a voice. I didn't see a specific thing. I think, I think I just heard the sound of silence. I just felt it in my soul, you see. There's not another way to put it."

"How long did it last?"

"I have no idea. Seemed like forever, or a nanosecond. It went south, I think, like a wind of light. Just gone. I turned around to the office and deleted my diagrams and my five-page explanation. I saw that it was mean, you see, to behave like that to my brothers and sisters. But I also know most of them are stupid. So then I quit my job. And that's that."

Grace chuckled softly. "You are a complicated person, aren't you, Alexander?"

He shrugged again. "Yeah, like that ever did me any good."

 Grace got up. "Look," she said, "I'll get us some water, okay?"

He didn't say anything. Grace walked into the small kitchen across the hallway and found two glasses. She poured water from the faucet, crushed the pill from her pocket into his glass, and came back to the living room.

"I know you are conflicted," she said, handing him the glass of water. She waited until he drank two times. "I might be able to help, but then again, what's the point. You'll never have to worry about your social abilities or holding a job anymore."

She sat down on the couch, and stuffed her notebook and pen in her backpack. She looked at him, sitting there all worried and confused inside. Depressed, even.

"Who are you again?" he asked, raising his eyes.

"I'm an angel, Alexander," she answered. She took off her jacket and relaxed. It was going to take about 20 minutes.

His lips started to get pale. "An angel?"

"Well, a special kind of angel," she admitted. "I lived in Heaven but I am now human like you."

"How come?" he asked.

"I asked to be sent down so I can help people better. See, from up there, you guys seemed so much in need of my help, with your prayers and all. Now of course I know that those prayers were pretty much lies."

"Ah," he said sadly, "I see you share my perspective on life. Then you understand how I am stuck between believing in Him, and then seeing His creation behaving so stupidly every day."

He drank the rest of the water, and wiped his mouth with the back of his hand. His face was white and circles started forming around his eyes.

"So you came to help me or what?" he retorted . "I didn't pray for it, you know."

"I do bring relief," she said. "I came to kill you. You will be in Heaven soon, and free of people, as you wish."

He stared at her in surprise. "What are you talking about?"

"Just relax," she said. "It won't be long now."

Grace sat down on the couch, as calm as she could be. She looked around the room and noticed the very large plasma TV. As she was staring at it, she saw something moving towards her. She turned, surprised, to see Alexander jumping out of his wheelchair and running towards her, obviously on two good and strong feet. She ducked and retreated to the other end of the couch.

Alexander grabbed her swollen leg with his long arm and pulled until her shoe came off. He threw it away and made another jump for her. Grace screamed in pain; she fought him but the surprise attack had caught her unprepared, and she was at a disadvantage. He managed to get on top of her and she could feel his dry, labored breath.

"You crazy bitch," he said, coughing. "I bet you didn't expect this. Yes, He cured me that night. I can walk again. Yeah, I didn't tell Father Dmitri. It was my little secret, and look, it came in handy."

Still pinning her to the couch, he reached for the coffee table.

"I'm calling the cops," he said. "Then you can tell them all about how you're an angel and all that crap."

Grace made an effort and freed her left leg from under him, and hit him hard in his side. He groaned but still managed to get the phone. She hit him again, making the phone fly across the room. They fell over the coffee table together, and he struggled to be on top again. Grace screamed - her arm was caught between the broken wood and Alexander's body. She gathered her strength and pulled it out.

He remained motionless though. The poison had numbed his muscles by now, and only his eyes were still fully alive. She got up from under him. It wasn't too late. She found her bag, pulled out the syringe and gave him the final shot, trying to ignore the pain in her left arm.

"Why?" he whispered. "Why does an angel kill?"

"I am not an angel anymore," she said. She found her shoe and swiftly put it back on .

He didn't say anything else after that. Grace waited, and when his eyes closed, she moved near him, holding his head to her chest, face to face, breathing with him. She saw it coming, his last breath, and was there to inhale it from his now dead lips. His vision of light became hers to keep forever.

▪▪▪ ▪ ı

"Ma?" Walker yelled, opening the door. She hated surprises.

"Ma?"

No answer. Walker felt that old terror in his heart, and visions of her lying dead started to dance in front of his eyes. He threw his coat on the couch and hurried towards her bedroom.

"Ma?" his voice now had a high pitch. He opened her bedroom door but the room was empty and silent. The bed covers were crumpled; the glass of water on the nightstand was still full.

The bathroom door was opened and she wasn't there either. Walker turned on his heels a couple of times, not sure what to do anymore. Maybe she had gone out, he feared. Maybe she was lost in the middle of Chelsea, and you know no one will bother to help her, not during rush hour.

"Ma!" he screamed again, and, just after that, he noticed the light in the guest bedroom. He pushed the door open, and there she was, all 92-pounds of her, sleeping in the unmade bed, shivering.

"Oh, God," Walker whispered. "Ma, wake up! Wake up!"

She opened her big brown eyes, the only things that still resembled the way she used to look. For a second, a warm smile appeared on her thin lips, and Walker cherished that small moment of recognition.

"What in the hell are you going on about?" she shrieked, trying to hit him with her weak hand. "I am taking my nap. Get the hell out of here."

"Ma, Ma," Walker said gently, "you're in the wrong bedroom. What happened? You're sleeping here, all cold, with no blanket."

"What are you talking about? I have always slept here. This is my house, mister. I know where my bedroom is, and don't you try to confuse me. I am sick of all you people trying to confuse me, I know what I am doing."

Walker went into her room and brought her robe, then helped her out of the bed. "Ma," he sighed, "you are getting worse. Did you do your exercises today?"

She shrugged, slowly walking into the kitchen.

"You have to do your exercises, Ma. The physical therapist is coming tomorrow. You know that you had a stroke, right?"

She looked at him with a blank stare.

"Will ya listen to me?" Walker started to lose his patience. "If you show no progress, they will give up on you. They will just let you sit here until you die. Do you understand? You need to try and exercise, and get better, so the insurance keeps paying for your medication."

She had the same blank stare, and Walker knew it was all part of the game in her brain, and that he shouldn't get mad at her because she was simply sick, but he couldn't help feeling angry at her - for being old, and sick, and not being there for him anymore, ever.

"I have to go out of town," Walker explained slowly. "I called the agency and they'll send Ginny to stay with you, okay? If you need somethin', you call me, okay?"

"Okay," she muttered . "Want some tea, honey?"

"I don't think I have time. I want to leave now so I can make it before rush hour."

"Okay," she repeated .

Walker went in his bedroom and packed a small bag with enough clean clothes for a few days. Toothbrush, hair comb, toothpaste, razor, blades, shaving cream. Ready to go anywhere.

He changed into grey slacks and a blue shirt, and fitted his suspenders over it. He passed by the bathroom mirror without even a glance toward it. He knew who he was, and he knew how he looked.

When he stopped by the kitchen again, his mom was drinking tea, sitting at the small table. She seemed even tinier, a child-like figure contoured against the sunlight. Walker went to kiss her forehead.

"I am going, Ma," he said. "There are frozen dinners in the fridge, okay? Please don't go out, just ask Ginny if you want something."

She perked up: "How about some of that calzone downstairs?"

"Sure, you can ask her when she stops by later, okay? Gotta go. Call my cell if you need anything, all right? And I'll be checkin' on ya."

She nodded, absent-minded again. Walker put on his long coat and grabbed his bag. "Love ya, Ma, take care," he waved at her as he opened the door,

The mug missed him by a few inches and splattered on the wall. "What the...?" he ducked quickly, avoiding a shower of hot tea.

"You bastard," she yelled. "You leave me alone. I raised you, I put a roof over your head, and now you're too good to get me a calzon'? Get out of my house! I don't want to see your ungrateful face!"

There was no reasoning with her when she got angry, Walker knew. It was a side effect of the stroke, her total change in personality. It wasn't her saying that, he knew in his mind; but her words still upset him, making him uncomfortable.

He slowly closed the door behind him and locked it. She would be fine, he reassured himself. The doctors said she was not a danger to herself and she could still do all basic tasks, enough to live alone with minimum supervision. She would be fine. She would be fine. With his heart heavy, he took the elevator to the garage.

5

Grace limped back to Rahway Avenue and walked north, passing tiny houses, a working crew, a group of teenagers and a mall. Her arm was hurting badly and she had to take care of it before going forward.

She finally reached the Trinitas Hospital and made her way to the Emergency Room door. There were only two other people waiting, an old man with an oxygen tube, and a young lady that stared blankly into space.

"I hurt my arm," she told the nice, maternal-looking nurse at the window.

"Oh, hon, sorry to hear," the nurse said. "Here, come in right this way, we'll do an X-Ray first."

As Grace waited in the small room, she fought back tears; she was mad and angry at herself. She had spent so much time researching everything about her victims, and preparing each stage of her trip, that she forgot real life always throws a curve. She had been arrogant, and had sinned by arrogantly thinking that she had it all figured out.

The paper on the bed crinkled as she moved. She held her backpack to her chest in a defensive position, shivering. There was nothing much in the room except for a small swivel chair and metal cabinets. Some syringes lay on one of them, and Grace eyed them with concern. In the corner, a creepy yellow trash bin labeled 'Hazard' had its cover crooked; a small patch of bloody bandage peeked out. Grace felt her stomach turn.

"It's not broken," said the doctor as soon as she entered the room. "That's good news."

Grace breathed a sigh of relief. "Thanks, that's really good news. Anything I can do for the pain?"

"It's just badly bruised. I'll give you a prescription for pain, please use it for 48 hours as needed. If it still hurts after that, call me back. Don't stress the arm. Try and keep it lifted and not moving. At home, use ice packs wrapped in a towel for comfort. You can also alternate warm wraps if needed."

"Got it, thanks."

"So, how did this happen?" asked the doctor, searching through mysterious things in her desk drawers.

"I stumbled while vacuuming," Grace said. "I hit the coffee table and I fell on my arm."

"Were you alone at the time?"

"Yes, yes, I was alone."

The doctor looked at her carefully, and Grace realized
what she was after.

"Oh," she laughed in submission, "no one abused me,
doctor. I don't have a husband of boyfriend. There was
really nobody else there."

"OK," said the doctor. "The injury could be consistent
with the fall you described. Sorry, I have to ask."

"It's okay," said Grace.

The doctor opened a jar of white cream and carefully
spread it on Grace's skin. The arm was red and black,
and slightly swollen from the wrist to the elbow.

"This should help a bit in the short run," she said. "Here's
the prescription. The nurse will be back to wrap things
up. Good luck, and call me if it doesn't look better in 48
hours."

"All right," Grace smiled.

The doctor left the room. Grace put her sweatshirt back on, shivering. Why was it always so cold in hospitals, she thought. As a little girl she had spent many nights in the emergency room, for burns, bruises, nose bleeds. Every little mishap turned into a trip to the hospital. They poked her and prodded her and hurt her even more, and they could never find any cause for her suffering. Until she figured that she was different, that she could feel pain a million times stronger than others. She learned to protect herself, to stay safe in the face of f anything that could have even slightly hurt her. She also learned to hide her pain from her mother and stop worrying her.

"Before you go, we'll have to draw a little blood, okay?" the maternal nurse told her entering the room. "And then I need some urine."

"Why?" Grace asked loudly. "I just have a bruise."

"Toxicology tests are standard procedure in this hospital."

Grace pulled back and hugged the sweatshirt around her.

"I don't think so," she said vehemently. "Please, stay away from me."

The nurse stopped in her tracks, surprised. "Honey," she said, "it's not going to hurt a bit, I promise. It's just procedure."

The pain had subsided considerably, and Grace felt her head clearing as well. Whatever am I doing here, she thought, looking around as if she had come out of a haze. To see it for what it was - a torture place, a witches' cauldron where people were sliced and diced and treated with evil-smelling potions; where light and dark were entangled in random diagnosis; a place built out of pain and despair, and the ridiculous will to live by people who should have long gone to the other side, but instead were clawing to every pill and herb they could, just to hang around one more day. Brick after brick of bad guesses and dead hopes. Walls painted with disinfected insides. Cold, wet, black rock all around.

"My blood is not for you to see," she hissed.

With a sudden move, she grabbed her backpack and pushed the nurse so forcefully she landed on the floor, and Grace ran out of the room and down the hallway, then out the emergency door.

■■

Detective Walker pulled into the St. John's church parking lot. His beat up car let out a noise of relief. It had been a long trip all the way to Alexandria, Virginia, a nearby suburb of Washington DC. He stepped out of the car and walked to the main door. It was late afternoon and all was quiet, except for the day care center on the other side of the building.

"Hello?" he said to nobody, trying to figure out where to go. There were announcements on the walls and several rooms down the hallway, and stairs going to the next floor.

"Detective Walker?" someone asked, and Walker turned around to see a tall man with white hair.

"Yes, that would be me," he answered and extended his hand.

"Father Halloway," said the man, and shook his hand with a soft grip. "Please, follow me. We've been waiting for you."

Walker followed him into a small room behind the kitchen. He passed about four paintings of Jesus and a couple of images of angels. Even the smaller shelves were adorned with tiny statues of the Virgin Mary and of unidentified saints. Walker tried to placate himself - he'd been in worse places.

Father O'Dell was sitting at a desk, typing furiously on a laptop. "Please, come in," he said, barely raising his eyes. "I need to finish this report in, like, 5 minutes. Please sit down," and he gestured in a distracted manner .

Walker sat down on a large wooden chair. "Go ahead, no worries," he said. "I totally get it about writing reports."

"Coffee?" asked Father Halloway. He seemed excited and nervous in the same time, and Walker reminded himself that this case had a way bigger meaning for churchgoers.

"Would love some," he answered. "It's been a long drive."

Father Halloway stepped into the kitchen.

"Nice little church you have here," said Walker loudly, just to break the silence.

"Thank you," said Father Halloway. "We're lucky to have a great community to support us."

Walker nodded. Like Bethesda, Alexandria was a rich suburb of the capital. Long ago, he had dated a woman from Northern Virginia and had spent many weekends driving around the area.

"OK," O'Dell said, "I am done. I apologize, Mr. Walker, but everyone wants to know what's going on." He shook the cell phone in his hand to make a point.

"So, what IS going on?" Walker asked, taking his cup of coffee from Father Halloway's hands.

O'Dell gave him a sharp look and for a second both men measured each other up. It was obvious to Walker that the priest's intelligence made up for his young age. He was, after all, chosen from many to conduct an investigation of great importance, so he was probably organized, methodical and had a good analytical sense.

"Well," said O'Dell, "I can try and start from the beginning. Two months ago, something happened. Several people reported seeing, hearing, or feeling God's presence, at the same time. Lots of them were in New York, and that's where the first reports came from, so we decided to take a look into it. Then others from New Jersey and Maryland came forward. So they sent me to talk with these people as well."

He stopped to take a sip from a glass of water on his desk. His light brown hair was cut short and clean, and his young face was smooth.

"And that's how come yesterday I met Mrs. Sherry. I talked with her for about an hour. It was extraordinary, the change in her. It is just... so inspiring, so miraculous. I only wish every person had her experience."

"Which part - when she hears God, or when she gets killed?" Walker asked, his sarcasm barely masked.

O'Dell smiled. "Not a believer, are you, Detective Walker?" he asked.

"A believer in what, exactly, Father? The institution, God, or people who think they have a direct line to Heaven?"

O'Dell weighed his answer and decided to let go. "These are the facts, Detective, whatever you think happened. This woman heard God telling her to come back to Him and His faith, and she followed the call. Yesterday when I visited she was giving away all the things she didn't find useful anymore. She truly believed now."

"Hmm," said Walker, "I am not sure I get this. Why give away things? Doesn't God allow for earthly possessions if you earned them honestly?"

"I actually wanted to talk with you about this," O'Dell said, "The psychology of these cases is extremely interesting. People experience a true vision and they understand their role in the Universe, so they want to live up to it. The way they interpret what happened varies wildly from person to person. Some start giving away everything, others start accumulating things they didn't care for before. Some decide to live in a cave, others decide it's a good time to go back home. There are yet others who decide to do nothing at all."

"Okay," said Walker, making short cryptic notes in his rugged notebook. "So, at what time exactly were you there yesterday?"

"I went in the morning, must have been eleven or so. We chatted for a while. She wanted absolution. A new start. So I said that's fine, and that I'll come back this morning. She told me to come very early because she was going to her in-laws' house to see her girls before school. So we decided on 6:00 AM, and I left."

"Anything you saw going on that was unusual?"

"There were some trucks loading furniture and other things she gave away. People came in and out of the house as we talked. Oh, and another thing. She had called a guy from the security company and disabled her alarm."

"Well," said Walker, "How convenient for the killer. Why in the world would she do that?"

O'Dell sighed and sipped some more of the water. "This is another common psychological effect," he said. "People feel secure. Too secure. They have no fear. They talk with strangers. They forget about the bad guys. They are assured that everything will be great, and they believe it. In the case of Mrs. Sherry, she was also planning to move out and sell the house. The way she went about it, she was trying to strip it down with a vengeance. . It reminded her of her past, I guess."

"Okay," said Walker, "So what happened this morning at 6:00?"

"Obviously I went there and there was no answer. By the way, I explained all this to the local police this morning. So I looked at the window - there were no curtains, and I saw her lying on the chair in an awkward position, and I called 911 from my cell phone. "

"No husband? Kids?"

"They had moved out the day before," said O'Dell. "The husband did not understand the change she was going through."

He proceeded to put the papers on his desk in order.

"I talked with Detective Mills," he said, his eyes lowered. "He is handling the investigation in Montgomery County. He is expecting you as well. I gave him all the details of my encounters with both Mr. Jackson and Mrs. Sherry. I'd be happy to repeat it all to you but he's got it recorded and filed. Basically they told me about their lives, and about their experience that night. There was nothing to suggest danger or enemies or anything like that."

"Hmm," Walker nodded. "Well, my boss says you can help me put together a profile of a potential killer, in case it was someone who is a believer."

"Yeah, I am working on that. I still need to get my head around all this. It's quite a stretch to imagine what motive someone could have."

"OK, well, I'm going to go talk with Detective Mills then, first thing tomorrow," Walker said and got up. "You're staying in town, right?"

"Yeah, sure, they wanted me to stay for a while until we finish the formalities. Father Halloway will put me up for the night. Just call the church, someone will get me if you need me."

He got up from his desk to shake Walker's hand, and that's when Walker noticed an interesting fact: O'Dell was a very short man.

"Yeah, sure, thanks," said Walker, coughing a bit from the surprise. "I only have one more question for now: when did you leave New York?"

"Yesterday, very early in the morning," he said, hurriedly stuffing papers in his suitcase. "I drove."

"Thanks a lot," said Walker and got up to leave. "I'll be in touch."

And he let the nice Father Halloway escort him back to the parking lot. This particular priest was old, weak and very tall. Walker felt safe.

6

The Internet totally believed the murder in New York and the one in Bethesda were connected; it totally did. There was a post on social sites that spread like wildfire, and it started with a quote from the Bible and it ended cursing the evil madman killer. You had to post it on your profile and use it to update your status and share it with all your hundreds of friends, or the Internet would have tagged you as a supporter of the devil. You had to pretend to agree with the content and pretend to believe even if on a regular day you didn't; you had to swear on your Mom's grave, cross your heart, and look up toward heaven; you had to follow the rituals the Internet had set. As always, it had managed to condense long and windy opinions into a 140-character perfect message. The Internet was great at that, at copyediting and generating short and effective ads for all situations. This one was also a preferred subject, a topic that the Internet itself helped propagate; faith, it was all about faith, and the Internet always said, all kinds of faith, no matter what your God was.

Matt Reed thought the message itself was not enough.
He forcefully wrote a new blog entry, fully demonizing
the mysterious killer. It was one of his best; it went on for
three full pages in print. In his direct, populist style that
had made him famous, he blasted the unholy with
tongues of fire. To him, the fifty-seven were almost
saints, chosen ones from a sea of half-believers. To
touch any of them with harmful intentions was to sin way
beyond your daily, petty sins. Maybe you thought you
were better than them; maybe you thought you were
better than God himself, going around like that with your
weapons and your dark thoughts, and your anger
clutching your black heart. Did you think you know
better? Because you don't. You cannot understand why
He touched these individuals, just as you cannot
understand the meaning of life or the origins of the
Universe. Just trust what fifty-seven people, complete
strangers from all walks of life, saw, heard or felt at the
exact same second.

Who could be so evil as to go directly against the ones
chosen by God? For sure there was a purpose in
choosing them; only it was not easily revealed to us. The
murders were an affront to God's will. The killer should
immediately cease, confess, repent, and pray that the

miserable corner of Hell he was going to be in for eternity could receive divine grace once in a while.

The others in the group of fifty-seven sheepishly came to his side. The old ladies gang was starting to freak out, and produced way too many biblical quotes, as if to fortify themselves against unseen evils. The scientists proceeded to collect details about the forensic evidence of the murders. The believers resigned themselves again to the present moment. Some theories appeared, were discussed, forwarded and addressed, and ultimately dismissed.

The killer was jealous of the divine experience the fifty-seven had witnessed. The killer had been sent by the devil, who was jealous that God had given us a message. The killer was a deranged person who thought that by killing the chosen ones, he would be somehow chosen as well. And he was jealous.

As the group posted, self-centered and oblivious, Matt Reed wrote again. The quote he posted was sad: it was about God passing by, and leaving only a gentle whisper in the wind. A dark streak of terror and despair was obvious in his post; Matt Reed suggested that the end was coming, that maybe God's visit was a sign of that. Otherwise, why choose some and then allow them to be killed? Maybe they were intended to die?

The Internet read all this carefully and wondered why was Matt so afraid. The Internet speculated that his faith was threatened somehow; and since he always was the one to best understand the fifty-seven, the Internet assumed that the identity of the killer must be so dark, so secret, so rooted in deep, ancient beliefs, that he was no mere devil.

After much discussion, the collective Internet decision emerged. It was something worse. The killer was an Angel of Death.

7

Chevy Chase, Maryland
Wednesday

Even the local police station looked rich, in this rich suburb of Washington, DC. The walls were recently painted , the phones were very new and looked like small UFO devices, and none of the chairs was broken. Walker sighed as he entered through the large glass door. The receptionist looked cute and well paid, judging by her wardrobe. Behind her, large coffee pots were brewing aromatic concoctions; pastries and fruit were on the counter.

"Can I help you, sir?" she said cheerfully.

"Well, first off, are you guys hiring? 'Cause I could really get used to this." He chuckled at his own joke. "No, seriously, I am Detective Walker, NYPD. Lookin' for Detective Mills."

"Oh," she laughed, "yes, he is waiting for you. One second."

Detective Mills was about the same age as Walker, but the differences between them were staggering. Healthy sun tan versus pale and shriveled; military-cut blond hair versus an unkempt pile of white curls; defined muscles versus floppy belly; confident smile versus depressed grimace. Walker shook Mills' hand, telling himself he could look like that if he really wanted to.

"I hear Father O'Dell already talked with you at length," he said, following Mills through the corridors of the police station.

"Yeah, we had him here for a few hours. We got all the details of what he saw and what he knew about the victims."

Mills stopped in front of an office and opened the door. It was a small room, but the large window lent an air of cleanliness and perfection. Even the papers on his desk were in order, Walker sulked. He almost didn't want to look for it, but there it was - the family picture with the beautiful wife and adorable son and daughter.

"Victims?" he asked. "Did you make the connection then?"

"Well, it was him who brought it up, really. He kept yammering about the other guy in New York. So we called you guys. Thought we might be on to something. You never know with these church fanatics running around."

Walker smiled; he was starting to like him a little.

"After O'Dell left," continued Mills, "we talked with a couple of priests from the Archdiocese of Washington. Everyone over there is kinda tight-lipped, you know. They don't want to come out and make any statements too early."

"Still, I hope they gave you a few pointers."

"We have the names of all those who, on June 2nd, saw, heard, or felt God walking by. There are fifty-seven of them, spread all over the East Coast from New York to Virginia Beach."

Walker sighed. "Maybe we jumped to conclusions here," he said. "Two out of fifty-seven is not a significant number. These crimes could be unrelated."

"We thought the same," admitted Mills. "But nevertheless we called each one of them at home and warned them to be careful because there might be a maniac out there. We reached all but three: one in DC; one in Elizabeth, New Jersey; and one in Baltimore, Maryland. For those, we asked the local police station to go and warn them in person."

"Very good thinking," Walker admitted. They were about five steps ahead of him, that's for sure.

Mills pushed one of the orderly stacks of paper towards him. "Here they are, what the Archdiocese gave us. Our Internet research department did an excellent job at getting some additional background information."

Walker looked through the neatly printed files. Various names and faces, old and young, disheveled and elegant. He scanned the pages for a while, looking for a pattern of sorts, but nothing came to him.

"Can I have a copy of these?" he asked. "I'm gonna need to look at them more carefully."

"That copy is yours, keep it," said Mills, all prepared. "We had people working on the files since yesterday morning."

"Yeah, you mentioned it, that Internet research department of yours."

Mills glanced back at him. "What, no web geeks in the NYPD?" he asked.

"Well, I think there's, like, two unshaved guys who, like, fix our computers and stuff. Not sure they are called a department."

"I bet downtown they have plenty of the computer nerds over there in Man-hattan," Mills teased with a southern accent.

"I guess," Walker shrugged. "Either way, I believe in what I see with my own two eyes, you know."

"I hear ya," Mills sighed. "Well, do whatever you people over there in Man-hattan do. We couldn't find any patterns. Victims were completely unrelated, have never met or talked. The New York man was outside of a bar when he saw God; the Bethesda woman was at a charity event in NYC. About 10 miles apart."

"I wonder if it had anything to do with timing. Like, maybe they were the first two to see it? In that order?"

"Nope, we checked," said Mills. "The woman saw it and then the man, and none of them was the first. The first was an old lady in Upper Manhattan. By the way, the blogger guy brought this up as well."

"The what?"

"Blogger guy. Goes by Matt Reed. He took a great interest in the 'phenomenon', as he calls it. The Internet is abuzz about the encounters with God, and he is the main voice. He is convinced the murders are related."

Walker smiled dismissively and made a mental note to check this out later. Apparently the time had come to see and read a "blog", whatever that was.

"Can you tell me anything about the Bethesda investigation?" he asked.

"Execution-style," Mills stated without any emotion whatsoever. . "Two injections, one to paralyze, the other to kill. Just like they do it for capital punishment. Did not find any fingerprints, syringes, footprints   or anything. The killer came through the back door, picked the lock easily, and walked in and waited for the victim. Alarm was off, since she was going kinda crazy and decided she didn't need it anymore."

"No cameras? On the street maybe? This is a pretty fancy neighborhood, right?"

"No, nothing. There's not much traffic. Funny thing is, they just passed this law in Maryland to put traffic cameras in residential areas such as this one. It takes effect tomorrow."

"Hmm, that's too bad. Not very helpful for Ms. Sherry."

"Yup," said Mills and leaned a bit over. "She was quite a beauty, you know. Even dead she had this... pose, you know. Like she was expecting the photographers."

"Listen," said Walker, "would ya mind terribly if I took a look at the crime scene?"

"No problem, I'll give you someone to take you there in the afternoon. Where are you staying?"

"Here's my cell number. I'll be staying at the Mountain View Inn in Springfield. I like to stay there every time I'm in DC," said Walker and got up to leave. "Thanks for everything, man. You've been very kind."

He shook Mills' strong hand and found his way back to the cute receptionist and out the door. If he remembered correctly, there was a nice Lebanese restaurant just down Wisconsin Avenue. Just the place to start reading the files Mills gave him, while waiting for the lunch hour.

■■ ı

After lunch, he found himself driving back to St. John's. Walker liked to not think too deep sometimes, and just follow the invisible pull of his intuition. It had worked many times during his long career. Unfortunately, his intuition and his brains had been totally useless when it came to women and relationships.

He pulled into the parking lot and was surprised to find it full. He parked at the far end, close to the wooded area, and squinted into the sunlight. I hope there aren't any coyotes around here, he thought. Nature freaked him out a bit.

Inside the church, groups of people moved around. There was a free ESL class upstairs, a prayer group in the main lobby, and some kind of kiddie show in the chapel. Everyone was smiling. The prayer group was serving punch. Walker felt utterly out of place again.

"Mr. Walker!" Father Halloway shouted from the other side of the lobby.

"Hi-ya," Walker shouted back. "Is Father O'Dell around?"

"He's in my office," said Father Halloway.

"Never mind, I'll go find him, I remember where it is."

Father Halloway raised his punch glass, smiling.

Walker found his way to the small kitchen and then the office. O'Dell was on the phone.

"M'am, I do understand," he was saying. "I don't have any information. The police is working the cases right now. I just wanted to warn you, please be careful.... Yeah, I know the police stopped by as well. I just... Yeah, sorry, I don't have any other information. I just... Hello?"

He hung up, sighing.

"Tough crowd?" asked Walker, taking a seat.

O'Dell laughed softly. "I guess after you hear God, other people's words are just not important anymore."

He stretched.

"Have you been in this office all day?" asked Walker.

"I was trying to call them, you know. I can't just stay idle. I thought maybe I can offer some encouragement. I don't know."

"I think that's laudable," said Walker.

O'Dell shrugged. He stepped into the kitchen and poured himself a cup of coffee. "Want some?" he asked.

"Sure, why not. I never saw a cup of coffee I could say No to."

They drank in silence. Walker studied him above his thick glasses. O'Dell looked exhausted; his hair was tussled and his beard was starting to show; his hand trembled when he put the cup down. Walker mentally erased him from the list of suspects. That left the list of suspects totally empty.

"So, how many did you call?" Walker asked.

"About twenty-five. Some weren't home so I left messages. I... lots of them asked if the killer is an Angel of Death. What an absurdity. I mean, it is almost a blasphemy. Whoever came up with that? I think they didn't believe me when I denied it."

"They're probably just scared," said Walker. "There could be a madman out to get them."

"Sometimes I think evil lives on the Internet," O'Dell whined. "Since this story broke, these people went online and came up with the most insane theories. Now it's the Angel of Death. No one knows how the name appeared. It's like evil itself sends messages sometimes, to create confusion and panic."

Walker nodded sympathetically. He'd heard worse.

"So, how long have you been a priest?" he asked.

"Oh, forever. I always knew I was meant to be in the service of the church. Ever since I was a little boy. I remember being at a mass once with my parents, and as I looked in awe at the statue of Jesus, this enormous feeling came over me. It was like it cleared my head, and I matured right there. I saw the Truth. I was touched."

"Hmm. Do you think that the fifty-seven people felt something similar?"

O'Dell shrugged. "It's different for everyone, I guess. To me, divinity is obvious and I feel it every day. To others, it is revealed when they are in distress. I, for one, took their story seriously from the beginning. I know it is unusual and against some of our own formal beliefs, but the changes in the witnesses were extraordinary. I mean, look at Ms. Sherry. She gave up everything she worked for. She confessed her marriage was on the rocks, her kids were spoiled. This is a woman who lived to show others how perfect she was."

"Both Jackson and Ms. Sherry had changed. What about the others? Any others that come to mind?"

O'Dell looked him in the eyes. It was easy to tell that he was a bright young man.

"If you are looking for a pattern, I can't help you much. Again, they are all different. Some gave up things, but most just continued to live. I guess these two were obvious because they turned their lives around by a hundred and eighty degrees. Lots of the others were regular people with pretty boring lives. They didn't change anything, they didn't get better, because they already were kinda all right."

"Maybe that is the pattern," said Walker. "Maybe the killer thinks the ones that were bad before don't deserve much."

"I don't think that makes much sense. I mean, they are good now, so what's not to like?"

"Well, I'm sure we'll figure it out. Right now, I don't know, it makes no sense whatsoever," Walker sighed and made a dismissive gesture. "I am tired as hell, my man."

He regretted saying 'hell' as soon as it departed his lips, and he made a funny, apologetic face that made O'Dell chuckle. The priest looked through the drawers of his desk and produced a small treasure - a cigarette.

"Huh," Walker queried, "well, who can blame you, after the day you've had. Got one to spare?"

O'Dell pulled a whole pack out of his desk. He opened the large window and invited Walker to come closer with a gesture. Walker lit up, realizing that was what he really needed.

"I quit smoking, you know," he said. "Two years ago, yeah," and he puffed away with great satisfaction.

"Well, I'm glad that's working for you?" O'Dell chuckled again.

They blew the smoke outside in unison. O'Dell stared at nothing.

"So what happened that made you reject the Lord?" he asked, and in the harsh sunlight his question seemed hard and accusatory.

"I do not reject the Lord," Walker protested feebly. "I reject the church as an institution. Just not a big fan of how they operate, you know."

"So what happened that made you reject the church?"

"I tell you what happened. I grew up, and then I grew a brain. And I read books, history books, and religious books. And then I made up my mind, as educated adults tend to do."

O'Dell carefully put out his cigarette outside of the window, and threw it away.

"We might not be perfect, Detective," he said. "But without an institution there would be anarchy. The word of God would be fragmented, corrupted and lost."

"Why do you think He came down?" Walker asked. "I mean, you must believe that it was really God, then why did He come down to visit us that night in June?"

"Who am I to know," O'Dell shrugged. "Maybe he was out for a walk or on his way to a picnic in the Universe, and we caught a glimpse of his sandals as he was passing by. There seems to be no clear message that he left us. A few people thought they heard him breath; others imagined words, but I find that questionable. I don't think He spoke at all. If He did, we'd have a coherent, unified statement. Instead, they all heard what they wanted to hear."

They leaned against the wall, looking out into the garden outside. O'Dell spoke softly.

"It is wonderful, and heartbreaking in the same time. I wish He'd, I don't know, done something extraordinary. A miracle, maybe. Or just a word. Anything."

"Well, he did turn fifty-seven people into believers, for starters. And who knows how many more strengthened their faith. I would think that's a miracle right there."

"Of course, of course, you're right. I am just left feeling… somewhat lonely, I guess."

Walker put out his cigarette. "We'll just have to figure it out, that's all. Once we do, all the pieces will fall into place. We find the murderer, we find the reason, and maybe we'll then find the higher meaning."

O'Dell smiled.

"I think I should call it a day," he decided. "I am going back to New York. I don't think they still need me here."

"Well, I recommend you join Father Halloway out there for a glass of punch. It looked quite tempting. You have my cell phone number, right? I'll be at the Mountain View Inn, a couple of miles from here, in case you need me."

"Will do. Have a blessed day, Detective."

Outside, the parking lot had emptied out. It was quiet as Walker tried to find his car. He passed the corner of the building and kept going toward the wooded area at the end of the lot. Suddenly, something moved swiftly ahead of him. He pulled out his gun instinctively.

A coyote looked at him, confused. It was light grey and medium-sized, and it was carrying a dead squirrel in its mouth. Walker and the coyote stared at each other for a long moment, then the coyote calmly retreated into the woods.

Walker silently put his gun back in the holder, an uneasy feeling swirling in his gut. Life and death had just passed by, distant and implacable, needing neither reason nor explanation.

8

Mt Airy, Maryland
Wednesday

Grace drove the rented Kia through the meandering one-
lane roads, passing farms, horses, cows, trees and
birds. The fall had colored all leaves in orange and red
shades. She felt happiness sneaking up on her, as it
often did. Ages ago, she had watched the colored leaves
from the Heavens and desired so ardently to be there.
Now, she was reduced to collecting small pieces of the
lost paradise.

She was lost, she realized. The shiny GPS embedded in
the board had gone crazy and apparently sent her in
circles. It was the third time she had ended up at the
same intersection. She looked at the map opened up on
the passenger seat. It was supposed to be the first left
ahead.

Finally she saw it, a street so narrow it was easy to miss.
The street sign was crooked and almost hidden by tree
branches. Grace turned left and followed the street down
the hill. Soon, she entered a townhouse development.
She drove slowly, looking for number 4354. It was quiet;

people were at work; the playground she passed was deserted as well.

She located the house, last one on the right. It looked like the others, except Grace could smell the purity and holiness inside. The windows were framed in red wood; so beautiful, she sighed.

She parked the car two spots down from the house. She knocked at the door; she could sense that no one was around.

"Who is it?" asked a voice inside.

"Mary Juarez?" Grace asked. "I am from the Archdiocese of New York."

The door opened to reveal a middle-aged woman. She had short black hair and an olive complexion she worked hard to hide with an expensive foundation. She wore high heels and a gray outfit. Coordinated eye shadow and nail polish. And all this just to stay inside the house all day.

"Maria," she said. "I am using Maria now, that's my real name."

"Nice to meet you, Maria," Grace smiled. "My name is Grace. I would like to talk with you a bit. Is it okay if I come in?"

"Sure," she said. She sounded tired, or disinterested. Like she had done some hard work, and was spent.

Grace stepped in and tried to close the door behind her, but the door wouldn't stay shut.

"Sorry," said Maria. "It's an old house." She pushed the door knob firmly and the door stayed shut.

Grace followed her into the living room. It was dark and badly furnished, to Grace's surprise. She sat down on the old couch.

"Would you like some coffee?" asked Maria. Her coffee cup was on the table.

"Oh, no, it's okay. Just maybe a glass of water, please."

Maria disappeared into the kitchen and came right back out holding the glass. She followed Grace's gaze towards the pictures on the mantel.

"Yeah, this was my parents' house," Maria explained. "I have an apartment in DC, right near Union Station. New, airy, with antique chairs and rugs. But since June I have found I can't stand it anymore. So I come here instead."

"That's understandable," said Grace, and sat on the small couch. "You have been through an extraordinary experience."

Maria started to cry, silently, still standing up. "I talk about it every day," she said. "But I never tire. I was forgiven, you see. For sins I didn't even knew I had. For being petty, vain, wanting stupid things, getting stupid things. He touched my forehead and I saw through it all."

Grace felt tears in her eyes as well. She had longed for His touch for so long.

"I wish it was me," Grace confessed. "But I knew I wasn't going to be chosen, not now, not   ever."

"Each and every one of us can redeem ourselves," said Maria with intensity. "Don't you see, we're part of Him. Even if we're sick, we can be healed. We need to be healed, we long to be healed."

"Not me," said Grace and sighed deeply. "I have stood against Him, and for that there is no redemption. That's the rule."

"But you're only human, you made a mistake. You didn't know any better. I am sure He'll forgive you, if you changed your ways."

"Ah, but there are only three things wrong with that. First, I am not entirely human, second, I do know better, and third, I did not change my ways. *I* did not forgive *Him*."

Maria gave her a piercing look. . She measured Grace up; petite, common, wearing baggy jeans, no makeup, unkempt brown hair.

"Uh-huh," Maria replied. "What exactly do you do at the diocese?"

"Enter data in the computer, keep the books, help the poor, things like that. I need to be in the church, you know. I miss Him so much."

Maria backed up slightly. "Well, I have to be somewhere. It was nice to meet you."

Grace smiled as she pulled out the gun. "Please don't move," she gently pleaded. Maria froze before she could reach the living room door.

"Pp...please," she implored. "What... what do you want?"

"Your last breath," Grace said sincerely. Unless it was for her survival, she preferred not to lie.

Maria gasped. "Are you crazy?"

"Don't worry. You will go straight to Heaven. It is wonderful there, everything you imagined and more. You will see this world for what it is, dry and impotent. Everything and everyone are as cold as stone, but people trick themselves into ignoring it. So harsh and frigid, and all that pain."

She saw that Maria was trying to think fast. "Look, I'm sorry if you had some problems in your life," she said. "Maybe I can help. Father Steven says maybe there is a reason why I was chosen."

Grace chuckled softly. "No one can help me, Mary. I am left longing for something I will never have again. I am giving you a gift - I am getting you out of this, and sending you to eternal happiness faster."

"Why me?" asked Maria, her voice quivering and her hands trembling.

"There were fifty-seven of you," Grace started, and her voice sounded condescending. "Each heard, saw or felt something different. Your ministers and priests can't make any sense of it, and treat it as yet another fake miracle. Only a handful of people felt Him breathing. You breathed it in. I need it. Sorry."

And she pulled the trigger, aiming for the upper body. The bullet went into the chest, through the lung and out through the back. Maria fell, gagging. There was less blood than Grace had expected, but it was starting to pool already.

She waited patiently, holding the woman's head on her knees. Grace had had no choice but to use her gun; her arm was still hurting, and Maria was a relatively young, strong person who would fight for her life. Grace hated using the gun; inevitably it produced gushing red blood, making her sick to her stomach and deep within her soul. Millennia ago, she had witnessed, in horror, the Son of God being tortured and crucified; blood everywhere, so much it had materialized on her gown, all the way in Heaven. It traveled fast, the blood, it was life given from above just as breath was given; blood carried power, and strength, and ancestors' tales; it had memories and dreams and it all came from the one sacred place, and it yearned to escape the humans' rocky bodies, and crawl back.

It had to be seven, maybe ten minutes before the heart stopped. Maria flailed her arms but her ability to resist was much impaired. Grace held her but did not try to restrain her; Grace's left arm was still hurting at the slightest touch. When it was time, she put her mouth on Maria's, and coldly collected the woman's last breath.

Grace changed her clothing right there. She had some blood spattered on her jeans and shoes. She took them off and put them in the bag; then pulled on a pair of sweat pants and sneakers.

As she was preparing to leave, the phone rang. She was almost out when the answering machine kicked in.

"Mary, this is Father O'Dell," she heard. "I was trying to get a hold of you since the police said they couldn't locate you at your apartment in DC. Here at the diocese we have your parents' address in the computer, so I thought I'd try you there. Anyway, there might be someone out to hurt the fifty-seven people who were part of the experience. Just thought I'd warn you so you'll be careful. I am actually in DC so I was planning to stop by later today. Hope to find you then."

Grace looked back. Maria was now surrounded by a small, dark pool of blood. Grace hurried, carefully closing the door behind her.

■■■

Walker plopped himself down on the hotel bed, sighing with relief. His old bones hurt. He had spent the afternoon at the Bethesda house, talking with the victim's husband and looking around, but no additional clues had presented themselves. A scene that could have been deleted from this movie, he thought. No value to it, and a few hours of his life wasted.

He put on the TV on the local news channel, and opened the Chinese food boxes he had picked up. His chopsticks froze in the air when he heard a familiar-sounding name.

"Matt Reed, the blogger who chronicled the June phenomenon, has written today about the connection between the two murders in New York and Washington,

DC and suggested that an 'Angel of Death' will be visiting all of the fifty-seven people who witnessed the experience, and kill them. This prediction has struck fear and panic among those targeted, and prompted church authorities to make announcements asking everyone to stay calm."

"I don't understand," said a woman identified as Sarah Dobbs, "we all felt goodness and light that night. Why would God give us that, if not for making us change our lives for the better? Why would he send an angel then to kill us?"

"Please, there is no Angel of Death, please," pleaded a priest identified as Father Hogue. "Please, continue to have faith and believe that God has a plan."

"I just have to say that Matt Reed knows things," said a young man interviewed on the street. "He gets this thing, you know. Of all the press and brouhaha, he was the only one that really understood what happened, and was calm and collected about it. So I tend to believe him, kinda. If I were one of the famous fifty-seven people - well, fifty-five now - I would watch my back carefully."

"Matt Reed, as always, refused to make any comment to the media on the grounds that mainstream news is irreversibly corrupt", concluded the TV reporter before moving on to the next story.

Walker continued to eat. He had to really understand this thing, too. There was no way around it. He remembered when it happened and it made some of the national news, but was mostly frowned upon by the large media. There were some interviews and some debates on TV, and a few of the people who had been through the experience were going to write books about how it changed their life. The Church's position was that true miracles happen only to those who are learned and therefore did not officially acknowledge this phenomenon, although several priests at local churches made it clear that they believed it.

Some of the fifty-seven had heartbreaking stories, and Walker specifically remembered one woman who had lost her son recently and was thinking of suicide, but after God whispered to her she made peace with her past and was ready to go on living.

Walker had never followed that news except when the TV was left on . Since the Church had been so powerfully against it, the story soon lost steam and credibility. Other stories about some of the fifty-seven cropped up, such as one that owed back-taxes, and another who had cheated on his wife. The fifty-seven themselves were never united as a whole; each acted and spoke for himself alone, and none of them could agree on what they saw or heard that night.

What Walker hadn't realized was that the story had kept on going strong, first in some local churches such as St. Mark's, and then on the Internet. The Internet, with its parallel universe of uncensored news, offered bulletin boards, chat rooms and blogs so that the fifty-seven could tell their stories one more time and answer questions, and make fans or enemies. The Internet judged them as a "phenomenon" and treated them as such, and it reflected the popular position more than the traditional media ever could.

Walker opened his briefcase and pulled out the files he got from the local police. He went straight for Matt Reed's writings - there were all printed orderly and marked with a date and time. He had started the blog a couple of days after the news broke:

"I demand that the media pays attention to this divine phenomenon. We have never, since the days when Jesus lived, seen such a close encounter with our Lord and with so many people at once. He is trying to tell us something. And he has chosen these particular people, why? There were a million others along the East Coast. Why them? If we can answer that, we will be closer to God's message."

No shit, thought Walker. Although the idea of talking with the remaining fifty-five people did not particularly enchant him, he thought it should be done. Whoever was murdering them had a motive, and an explanation.

He took out his cell phone and dialed his office in New York. "Hey, Linda, hon," he said cheerfully. "It's Sieg. Fine, fine. I'm still in DC but will probably come home tomorrow. Listen, can you patch me through one of those nerds in the computer lab? I don't care which one, they all look the same to me. Thanks, hon."

"IT, Kevin here," said a masculine voice.

"Oh hey-ya Kevin," Walker mumbled. "Hey listen, do you know a lot about the Internet and how it works and stuff?"

"I sure do, Detective," laughed Kevin. "What do you need?"

"Well there is this guy who writes a … blog, yeah. Can we find out who he is, where he's blogging from, his real name, things like that?"

"We can try. Usually we pick up at least some traces, even if they are very good at hiding. What can you tell me about it?"

Walker read aloud the blog's URL, painstakingly spelling each letter and backslash.

"Oh, the Reed guy," Kevin said when he was done. "Why didn't you say so? I read his blog already."

"Well, goody for you and me then," Walker remarked. "I'd just like to know who he is and what he does, you know, nothing major."

"No problem, will do, Detective."

Walker put aside the empty Chinese food boxes and lay down on the bed, files spread around him, photos looking up at him. Old, young, women, men, black and white. All alone at the moment when the skies had opened up. All witnesses to something extraordinary. He tried to imagine how they felt, sitting there in a normal minute of a normal hour, only to be swept away and shown Heaven through a peephole. But, hard as he tried, he couldn't do it. Nothing in his life had born any resemblance to a supernatural experience. Maybe he wasn't a chosen one, or a very perceptive one when it came to these things. He focused so much on the details, on the day-to-day tasks, on the task at hand; focused on doing something rather than talking or dreaming or wondering about it.

He had just about finished reading the files of the two victims, when his cell phone rang. It was Mills.

"There was another murder," he said. "A woman in Mt. Airy. Gun wound to the upper body."

"One of the fifty-seven? I don't remember anyone from Mt. Airy."

"Yeah, she was one of them, but this is her parents' house. Mary Juarez. Come on down and take a look if you want. O'Dell is here as well."

Walker entered the address in his GPS with one hand while looking for his coat and car keys. Someone was definitely doing the work of the Angel of Death.

■■

It was late when Walker arrived in Mt. Airy. Mills greeted him and showed him inside.

"By the way," he grinned, "O'Dell found the body. He's pretty shaken."

They looked at each other and smiled in acknowledgement. . Finding two bodies in two days was quite a streak of bad luck for any civilian.

The house was small and old, and Walker had a little trouble getting by all the cops inside. Time to stop eating all that pizza, he thought to himself, sucking his stomach in as he passed through the dimly-lit hallway.

The woman's body lay in a pool of blood in the living room. Something was a bit off, he sensed immediately. Maybe the way her head had fallen, awkwardly angular to the body. He looked as close as he could.

"Look here," he told Mills. "The gun shot came from the front, yet her head is tilted to the right. You'd think the impact made her head go backwards and straight."

"Hmm…," said Mills, and he kneeled down to get a better view. "I guess we can wait for the doc's report to be sure.

But are you saying her head was moved after she was shot?"

"I don't know, might be. Why would the head be moved though? You shoot someone and then you, what, cradle their head in your lap as they die? But, Jackson had an unusual position as well."

They both stood up, sighing.

"No fingerprints, no gun. Waiting for the lab to confirm but looks like it's the same as the one used in New York. We're starting to talk with her friends, husband, all that," said Mills.

"Yeah, good, solid police work always pays off. I ain't buying the Angel of Death theory."

"Phhhfft," Mills dismissed it. "Betcha this 'angel' is just another crazy with a gun."

Walker looked around at the scene. Nothing seemed out of place; no signs of struggle. On the table, an open newspaper and a cup of coffee, half full.

"Looks like she opened the door and let the killer in. Maybe someone she knows. Where was the husband?"

"He's in Miami. Business trip. He's some big shot CEO of something or other."

"So she was rich? Just like the Bethesda woman?"

"Yeah, they were quite well off. But your victim in New York wasn't rich at all, so I'm not sure that's the pattern we're looking for."

"I know, I know,' mumbled Walker. "Just fishin' for somethin'."

He saw O'Dell in the dining room. "I'll go talk with him," he told Mills. Mills nodded.

"I thought you were going back to New York," Walker said loudly, sitting down near O'Dell.

"Yeah, well, I stopped to see this woman on the way. She was dead when I got here. Blood all over."

He looked exhausted and his blue eyes had lost their sparkle. "I'm sorry," he said, covering his face with his hands. "This is the second dead body I find in two days. I am going to need some time to work this out."

"So what happened?" Walker asked sympathetically, totally convinced by now that O'Dell was innocent.

"I stopped by, the door was ajar, I knocked, went in, and there she was. I called 911."

O'Dell sighed heavily. "I don't understand it," he said in almost a whisper. "I have prayed and I have tried to work so hard, and I cannot understand why anyone would target these people. What kind of twisted mind does something like this?"

"That's why we're here, Father," said Walker. "We'll catch him, don't you worry. That's what we do."

"I need to get away from here," he said and got up. "I need some time, please."

"Of course," said Walker. "Look, how 'bout I'll take you back to my hotel. Stay the night, calm down, get a good night's sleep. We'll talk in the morning."

"Okay," O'Dell agreed. "Whatever."

Walker turned back towards the living room and signaled Mills goodbye. Mills nodded and came over.

"Come to my office tomorrow morning," said Mills. "I'll talk with the Captain. Bring O'Dell too. We need to regroup and re-think our strategy. Now let me see you out, it's madness here. I see all seven homicide detectives showed up and are lookin' to get busy. You gotta understand - we rarely have murders here in Montgomery County."

They walked out through the crowded hallway.

"Will have more details from Crime Scene tomorrow," said Mills. "All I know now is that it was a .38 special, and that the wound was not instantly mortal. Doctor says there were 7-10 minutes before she died."

"He is taking his time," Walker mumbled.

He helped O'Dell into the car and started driving, deep in thought.

9

The Internet went totally crazy when the third murder hit the news. Three in three days, and the police had nothing, not one clue, not one witness, not even one of those sketches of suspects to show on TV. No cars had been observed at the scene. No fingerprints, no hair, no skin, no DNA.

The Angel of Death had superpowers, the Internet decided. He flew in through the night, silent, with big, dark wings whooshing from above. He held his hand out towards the victims, and they fell, like being shot from a revolver. They flapped about helplessly, with terror in their eyes. They saw their life pass by and their souls leaving their bodies and fleeing into the Angel's hand. And then they died.

The real question is: Why? Matt Reed wrote in his blog. If we answer this question, we will find the motive and then we will understand the Angel, and through him, God's own will.

For money, the logical ones said.

But the Angel, with his big, dark wings, did not take anything. He did not want anything from his victims except for their souls.

Because they were sinners once, the old ladies' group argued.

Each of the fifty-four panicked in his or her own way, battling old demons. Who had not sinned amongst them? They all had things they were ashamed of, big and small, important or not. For sure the Angel knew all of them, and had a neat list of the naughty and the nice. None of them felt they honestly belong on the nice list.

A rush of confessions followed. Everyone called their pastor, went to their church, prayed, and posted all of this as their status on the social networks online. The Internet took in this information and filed it. It also offered, through its search engines, cleansing rituals and spells to help rid themselves of sins and shame. To be born again into purity and light, innocent as a newborn baby. Many clicked on the links.

10

Walker dreamed of Brooklyn; he was walking home on an empty street, in the dark. A woman screamed; a baby cried; a shadow appeared in front of him. He tried to run but his feet wouldn't listen. He struggled to reach out and he finally did it, putting his hand on the person's shoulder. She turned; she was stunningly beautiful, with baby blue eyes and waves of blonde hair flowing around her face. "Ma?" he asked. They were now in his childhood home, a cramped 2-bedroom in Chelsea. "Come in," he told his mother, who was standing now in the doorway. "Come in, will ya? Why ya sitting out there for?" She hesitated. Her hair was now brown and her eyes dark. "Come in, Ma," Walker said again. "Look, there's a coyote coming for you."

He woke up in a sweat. It was exactly 3:00 AM. He sighed and turned around in bed. He knew he would not be able to sleep again that night.

He waited until 6:30 before calling home. His mom liked to wake up early every morning, as if she were still young and taking care of the house and the three small children.

"Ma?" he asked.

"Yeah?"

Her voice sounded tired.

"It's me, Sieg," he said.

"Who?"

"Sieg, your son. How are ya, Ma?"

"Okay," she answered hesitantly, and he wasn't sure if she understood whom she was talking to,

"Did you have a nice breakfast yet?"

"Yeah, yeah, I had my toast and my coffee, yeah."

"How are you feeling, Ma? Are you feeling all right?"

"Sure, sure, I'm all right. But Ginny is being mean to me, you know."   She suddenly became talkative. "She took my laundry. I said don't do my laundry, Ginny, but she still took it. I don't know why. I wanted to pack it in the car. I mean, I am leaving here soon. I'll just do the laundry when I get where I am going."

"Where are you going, Ma?" Walker asked calmly.

She didn't answer. Walker knew the expression on her face when rational questions were asked; she stared blankly and refused to acknowledge anything that her damaged brain could not handle.

"Look, don't go anywhere until I get home, okay? Then we'll get in the car and together we'll drive wherever you want to go, okay?"

"Okay, but you need to talk with Ginny. I need to pack my bags, and she took my laundry!" She was starting to get angry, and Walker knew that wasn't good for her.

"I'll talk with Ginny, Ma, don't you worry. Love you, Ma. Try and have a great day, okay?"

"I dreamed of your Pa, Ziggy," she said suddenly. "He looked good, you know, like when we first met. So strong and handsome. I dreamed that he was fixing my car. He taught me how to fix cars, you know. He loved them cars."

"I know, Ma, I know."

"One time we even raced, did I tell you?"

He didn't answer. Of course she had told him the story a million times, but he let her do it one more time. She had condensed her life into a few anecdotes that she told over and over; it gave her great satisfaction.

"I love you, Ziggy," she said in a moment of clarity. "You take care of yourself, baby."

She hung up, and Walker realized that tears were streaming down his cheeks.

■■■ ■

O'Dell couldn't fall asleep until about 3:00 AM; as soon as he did, he dreamed of someone sneaking into bed with him; he dared not look who it was. The person was smooth and delicate and put her arms around him gently. Is it an intruder? he feared. Will she kill me just to steal my money? He was too afraid to open his eyes and look at her; he pretended to sleep. He felt her breath close to his ear and he held his own. Her hand touched his left side, and he felt it starting to squeeze, harder and harder, inside of his chest.

He woke up and immediately checked himself; sure enough, his chest was on fire. He searched for his pills and swallowed two, plus a Melatonin. He went back to bed, exhausted.

■■

Grace pulled into the parking of the New Joy Church. It was almost midnight. She had stopped for dinner at a family restaurant in Frederick, MD; she had soup and salad; she couldn't tell how it tasted. Miss Ellie, the owner, kept coming over to the table and chit-chatting, carrying a large pot of coffee. Two disgruntled middle-aged men were having chicken pot pie at the next table. An elderly couple was enjoying pancakes. It was clear that everybody was a regular, and Grace was the mystery guest Miss Ellie wanted to find out about. She tried to blend in, chat back, pretend to be shy, answer questions vaguely, even joke. One of the men started to ogle her; even with her plain clothes and dyed hair, people could still tell she was a beauty, if they looked long enough. Fortunately a family with a little boy came in, and Miss Ellie departed to talk with the boy about wrestling shows. The food must have been good, judging by how everyone was stuffing their faces, and by the strong smells from the kitchen. Grace finished everything on her plate, bagged a leftover piece of bread, paid cash and left a large tip. The little boy waved at her as she walked out into the cold night. She cringed.

Her limp had worsened, and her toe was now almost breaking through her shoes. It did not hurt anymore; it had died into human flesh.

The rented Kia had lasted pretty well through all the day's trips. She had filled it up just as she entered Baltimore and veered off I-95, even though by then, her impatience had grown almost unbearable.

The church was one of the few that stayed open all night. The parking lot was empty and Grace chose a place close to the door but away from the street light. She walked in, like a traveler looking for water after days in the hottest desert; she pushed the door and found herself in a small worship room. The receding lights were on a low-hanging ceiling; red curtains covered the two windows; the podium was bare, and behind it the only decoration was a large sign with the church name. She sat down in the last pew, shaking.

It took minutes before she could calm down completely. Images of the dead bodies were dancing in front of her eyes. She squeezed her eyes shut, to no avail. To kill was to go against every fiber of her being; her skin was burning from the inside because she had had to do it. She already felt like she was roasting in hell, surrounded by red-eyed demons poking her with sharp stakes. To kill was unnatural, un-human, and definitely not divine. To bear life, to nurture it, to love it, that was what God required. To reach out, to touch, to build, to continue, that's what He wanted.

She prayed in uncontrollable bursts, crying. She just let her pain pour out, without trying to put it in words or explain it, or deal with it. She was clutching her bruised arm unconsciously. It was getting worse, as it usually happened when her delicate body was hurt. It took a long time to heal, as if her cells were made of a different material. And maybe they were - the tests and doctors had never figured it out.

She felt raw inside, an open wound; her feelings boiling and in turmoil. Harmony, control, and beauty were distant memories.

After a while, she understood that there would be no answer that night either. She gathered all her strength. It had to be done. It had to be done, she told herself. She felt her anger and hatred and disgust come back and lift her off the bench.

It was a little after 3:00 AM when she got back in the car and started driving toward Ocean City. Under the faint light in the car, she could see that her left arm was now gray and rock hard.

11

Thursday morning
Chevy Chase, MD

"I tell ya right now," Walker said, biting into a large biscuit with gravy, "no offense, but if saw God, I would ask him a favor, you know? Like, can I have a better job? Can you make me win the lottery?"

Mills slapped his knees, laughing. Walker was on a roll making jokes all morning at breakfast.

"I'm always such a jerk when I don't sleep," Walker commented.

Just then O'Dell walked into the police station cafeteria, wearing the same clothes as the night before, as Walker astutely observed.

"I did the best I could," he said as soon as he sat down. "Here's my profile of the so-called Angel of Death. He's definitely a believer - no matter what religion. A person who does not believe simply would not bother murdering these people."

"Hear, hear," Walker punctuated, raising his coffee cup. Mills chuckled.

"Then," continued O'Dell, "how did he know their addresses? How did he know that Mary was at her parents' house? And more importantly, what did he tell Mary to have her trust him and let him in?"

He paused for effect.

"I think this man is an insider."

Walker and Mills stopped smirking. "You mean, a man of the cloth?"

"Yes," O'Dell nodded. "Maybe one of these priests who go around our orders and support the phenomenon openly. A rebel of sorts."

"It makes sense," Walker agreed. "I think we should look at who has access to the documents of the fifty-seven. Who knows their addresses and phone numbers, and can see the files the church made for each of them."

"Or someone who has their attention and can get access to them, like that blogger guy," Mills suggested.

"No," O'Dell insisted. "No, it has to be an insider. Someone like this cannot stay away from the church - he is attracted to it, needs to be involved with it every day. Your blogger admits to having never stepped into a church in his whole life."

Walker and Mills looked at each other, thinking the same thing. This was NOT what their bosses and the archdiocese wanted to hear.

Mills' phone beeped once. "Text message," he explained, looking all cool to Walker, who was not sure what that was. "Huh," he said, reading. "They found fingerprints... many. Everywhere around the Mt Airy and the Bethesda house."

"Excellent!" exclaimed Walker. "Now we're getting somewhere."

"Except..." said Mills, "they're blank."

"What in the hell do you mean, blank?"

"I mean, there are traces of fingers but the indentations are missing."

"Like, he cleaned them?"

"No, no, if he had cleaned them, then the finger traces would be smudged. These are clear, only blank inside. My guy says these are the clearest fingerprints he's ever seen - the most identifiable - only they cannot be identified."

"Did he burn his fingers with acid, or something like that?" O'Dell asked.

"Could be," Mills mused thoughtfully. "Listen, Father, do angels have fingerprints?"

Both Walker and O'Dell looked at him like he was crazy.

"Never mind," he mumbled. "He probably burned his fingers. How about this," he said trying to regain his credibility, "I'll go upstairs and get a list of all church people with access to the files, and make sure we have fingerprints on all of them?"

"Now that sounds like a plan," Walker approved, a little too enthusiastically. "We'll be in your office in a bit. Let me finish this good Southern feast here."

Mills rushed his good-byes. Walker refused to let doubt even enter his mind.

"We'll find him," he reassured O'Dell. O'Dell nodded vigorously.

Walker's phone emitted a short beep as well. "I'll be damned," he laughed, amused to no end, "I think I got me one of those text messages too. Where's Mills to see me all immersed in this new technology?"

"It's not that new," O'Dell smiled. "Here, I'll help you read it," he offered, watching Walker awkwardly handling his phone "It's from a Kevin?" he said.

"Kevin? Oh, the computer guy, of course. No one else I know in the whole wide world would ever think of 'texting' me."

"It says it was very hard but he found the blogger. Real name is Michael Dumfry and he lives in Ocean City, Maryland."

■■

The warm weather was gone; a persistent, cold rain was gripping them now.

"Feels like November, finally," Walker commented. He turned off his cell phone and put it back in his pocket. Third time calling Michael Dumfry, with no luck.

They had re-grouped in Mills' office. Mills had news - another victim had been found in New Jersey. Local authorities couldn't reach him to warn him, so they stopped by and found his body in the house.

"Same poison as in Bethesda," said Mills. "Same blank fingerprints."

"Same killer," muttered O'Dell. He looked pale and tired. He hadn't eaten much at breakfast; he was fasting, he explained, while resisting Walker's offers of bacon and eggs and waffles.

"Apparently there was a fight. The man jumped out of his wheelchair and attacked the killer. The coffee table was broken, the phone smashed."

"Then there should be fibers, hair, something?"

"They found the same artificial hair as in New York, and fibers from the same common sweatshirt. No footprints. One thing they tell me," said Mills rocking in his chair, "is that the fingerprints belong to small, narrow fingers. Look." He gave some photos to Walker.

"I would even say... delicate fingers," Walker added . "Are you thinking what I'm thinking? A woman?"

Mills nodded. "Very possible. That would explain the short stature as well."

He pulled some more papers from underneath the pile of files on his desk.

"I called the Archdiocese in New York City," he said. "Then the one here in D.C. They came up with a short list of people who had seen all the records of the fifty-seven. Only three women amongst them."

"Did anybody check if they have fingerprints?" O'Dell asked, and it didn't sound naïve.

"Yeah, all have fingerprints on file. They were fingerprinted when they were hired."

Walker slurped his coffee. "Well, let's talk with these ladies. Two in D.C., one in New York?"

"Correct. Lisa Dwayne, Karen Cooley, Grace Jarzinski."

"Oh, oh," O'Dell shouted, "oh, I know Grace. She helps us with clerical work and some hospitality work. She is the sweetest, nicest, most devout person you'll find living on Earth."

"I am calling right now and inviting the DC ladies over here," said Mills. "We need to see if they fit our profile."

11

Ocean City, MD
Thursday morning

Grace turned into the parking lot off the Coastal Highway. It was on 15th Street, close to the Boardwalk but on the quiet Bay side. She looked at the apartment building; kind of old but with a certain charm, all wood and surrounded by greenery. The balconies were large and furnished with old armchairs, potted plants and smiling gnomes.

She climbed the stairs to the second floor, limping along. She had rented an apartment on the top floor. It was easy; in November, especially during the week, demand was very low.

The apartment looked small but well-maintained, with wood paneling and an ocean theme all around. Shells, tiny boats and marine scenes everywhere; a large navigation wheel served as the main attraction in the living room.

Grace unpacked her bags and headed straight for the bathroom. She turned on the shower and stepped in, rubbing her sore left arm. She washed off the fake brown color from her hair, and took out her contact lenses. By the time she had finished, her beautiful, long blond hair skimmed her shoulders, and her intense blue eyes had shaken off the humble expression she had worn all week. She stood straight in front of the mirror as she chose her clothes - white, tight jeans, black lace top, black jacket. Added pearls, and pearl stud earrings. Put on foundation, makeup and lipstick.

Every time she looked in a mirror, she saw herself in her true form, a tall, straight, white bolt of light, her majestic wings reaching outwards and upwards. But lately she saw herself rigid, and hardened, and gray; she was becoming more and more human, with sins weighing on her and imprisoning her in yet another cold rock, to join those she could not stand. Her foot and her arm were now completely lost to human form, never to return to their heavenly matter. The rock was heavy, pulling her down, into the ground, where humans tended to go after their short, painful lives. Her light was flickering, and her wings were gone.

She listened carefully; there was some noise from next door, maybe someone was also taking a shower. She quickly finished, then packed her old clothes in a large garbage bag. She found her shoes and left, carrying the bag with her.

She knocked at the door next to hers, and waited. A minute later, a surprised man opened the door. He was almost handsome, his hair curly and a bit long, his hands clean and neat; he wore modest clothes.

"Wow," he said. "I thought I was imagining things. No one has knocked at my door since last summer's Russian kids when they got drunk."

Grace laughed, throwing her head back and revealing her perfect teeth.

"I'm sorry," she said, "I have moved in next door and I was wondering where I take the garbage out. I heard some noises so I was hoping someone was home."

"Well, I am the only permanent resident in the building. All other apartments are only rented during the summer."

"By Russian workers, I get it," she laughed again. "I plan to stay for a while. So I am glad I have a neighbor."

The man's smile suddenly disappeared. "I am mostly gone, you know. Work, things like that."

"I'm Grace," she said and extended her hand.

"Mike," said the man. He hesitated before shaking her hand. "So, Grace, the garbage cans are behind the building, over there." He made a vague gesture. "Nice to meet you."

"Thanks, Mike. Nice to meet you too."

The door closed fast and Grace found herself standing there alone, wearing pearls and makeup and all that. She impatiently turned around, found the garbage dumpsters and threw the bag in. There wasn't much time left. She had to get to him, one way or another.

Back in her apartment, she decided she had made all the wrong choices. She changed fast; put on jeans and a white t-shirt. Cleaned up the makeup and lipstick, and pulled her hair into a ponytail. Took her tool bag with her, just in case.

She knocked at Mike's door again. She could hear the TV faintly in the background. She heard shuffling but he didn't open. She waited for a few minutes, then took out her lock pick and forced the lock. She pushed the door open with brute force.

"Sit down, Michael," she commanded, and closed the door behind her. "We need to talk."

■■■■■■■■■■■■■■■■■■■■■■■■■■■■■■■■■■■■■■■ ι

He fell into the armchair. He was wearing an old, gray robe which comically showcased his hairy legs when he sat down. Grace looked around: old sofa, old TV, a bowl of chips on the old coffee table.

"So what's your sin?" she asked. "Obviously, you're not rich."

"My sin?" he mumbled.

"All of you touched by God that night had some kind of shady stuff going on."

"Ah," he sighed in exasperation, "so that's what this is about. You're one of those fanatics who were following us anywhere. Never had someone break into my house before though."

"Tell me, Michael, tell me all about what happened. I need to know."

He smiled, like he had heard this many times before. Grace watched as he was trying to decide what to do, but, as always, the thought of his experience suppressed everything else, and he could not help but start talking about it even if the words seemed to be forced out through his clenched teeth.

"I was driving home from Easton. I was just crossing the bridge into Ocean City, when I somehow felt I had left the car and was walking straight into this... cloud of white light. I looked around and saw Him, or saw something that reminded me of Him. I recognized Him at once, like I had known His face forever but somehow had forgotten it, in the muddiness of my stupid little life. I can't describe it, you know. I've tried. It was just, like, so obvious to me."

Grace wiped a tear from her cheek. "Keep going," she said gently. "I know what you mean. We recognize ourselves in Him, and we see Him in us. We are all His children."

"I kept walking, and it was as if we were walking together. I was going in and out of my own self, as if I was me and then I was within Him, and then I was just me again. I was happy, gloriously happy like I have never been before, ever. I didn't want it to ever end, this walk. But then it did, and I found myself in my car again, and the night sky was black as usual."

He stopped, and remained lost in thought.

"Thank you," said Grace. "Thank you."

He shrugged. "You could have read it online. No need to break into my house."

"Yeah, I did," she said, and got up to get some water from the small kitchen. "But I love hearing it from a person. It connects us. A lost science since everyone went online."

"The whole thing left me even lonelier," said Michael. "At least before I lived my life despising people from a distance, and drew some satisfaction from seeing them fail because of stupidity and weakness. Now I see how wrong I was, I realize that I was doing bad simply by not doing anything good."

"Evil is the absence of good, they say," commented Grace, drinking from her glass and handing Michael another one. "So that's your guilt – the venial sins. Not helping, not empathizing, not reaching. Am I right?"

"I've been hurt," he admitted. "I drove over the Bay Bridge one afternoon, and there was so much traffic, and a lane was marked as closed but there was nobody on it. I joked with my wife about it, but after a while we both thought it wouldn't be such a crazy idea to take it. We were stuck for 40 minutes in the same damned spot, and no cars at all on that closed lane. She said Do it, Mike. Screw these losers. I want to get to the beach. And as I swerved in, another car came from the opposite direction and hit us on the right side, where she was. And she died right there."

Grace glanced at her watch. It was already 8:00 AM. She had only a few hours left. But Michael had taken his head in his hands and started talking again.

"I couldn't talk for a while. I felt I had nothing to say to anybody. I was done, spent, I just wanted to die. I mean, we were married only a few months. We were planning on having kids, you know."

He raised his head and sipped some water. "Do you have kids, Grace?"

She threw herself out of the chair, eyes ablaze, fists clenched. She then realized that it was just a question, just a normal question that might come up in any normal conversation. She turned around and looked out of the window until her cheeks lost their blush.

"I can tell you about pain too, Michael. Pain is to carry your baby in your body for twenty-five weeks, and be so blissful and blinded by this divine and wonderful gift, that you don't realize that two drunken thugs follow you on the street, and push you into a dark alley and hit you and rob you, and then stab you by accident or to have fun, and leave you there dying, not just you, but the baby too, and all you hear now is her heart beat slowing down as the pool of red blood gets bigger, and you try to scream but you can't, and no one comes. That is pain, Michael."

He looked at her in surprise. "Who are you?" he asked. "What are you after? I thought you were one of those religious kooks, but you can't be, not with that kind of anger inside you."

"I asked to be sent to Earth and He let me come. I came full of hope and good intentions. I came as an answer to the prayers of a woman who was praying so hard for a child. I lived, and loved, and helped, and believed. Until that day that shadowed my soul forever. I will never be able to forgive Him for letting it happen, even though I understand that this is part of life here, and I understand, in my mind, how it works; but in my heart none of those matters, except the pain I am left to live with, forever."

"You will be reunited with your child in Heaven, Grace," he said softly. "I am sure you know that."

She shrugged, keeping her eyes to the ground. "It's not likely I'll ever make it back there. I was angry. I stood up to God, and this is a sin that it is not ever forgiven. Me and my child, we will be separated by an eternity of space and time."

She walked across the room and stared out of the window again. There was no movement outside; no cars passing on the quiet street, nobody else in the whole building or the one close by; she shivered, suddenly cold in the emptiness and loneliness around her.

"This world is a dry rock with tiny specs of gold," she said. "I hit my head and my soul everywhere I walk. The trees and the blue sky are an illusion. There is no beauty, only tiny specs of mirrors. This world is injured and constantly battered by freezing winds. I doubt everything now, after living here for twenty years. I only have one thing to cling to for my sanity - the love for my child."

She turned around and sat down again. Her hands were shaking.

"I'm sorry," said Michael. "I'm so sorry for your terrible loss. Is that why you kill people?"

She looked at him. Smart boy, she thought.

"How do you know?" she asked.

"Police called yesterday to warn me that someone might be targeting people in our unusual group," he answered. "Online, we called him the Angel of Death. I kind of imagined a burly guy with a big cross around his neck and insane eyes. But I guess it was you, huh?"

"I hope you're not blogging this," she smiled.

"Ah, so we're both all out of secrets then," he smiled too. "You know I am Matt Reed. I can't help it. For many years, I did not talk much. But after that night, He gave me the tongues of fire. I can't stop writing about it. And I don't think that I helped them much either. I think I failed them, and I failed Him in the mission he gave me."

He got up and paced between the couch and the dining table.

"They looked to me for an answer, for an explanation. Why did He come? Why did He choose us to reveal His presence? What message did He leave us? And I do not know. I tried to deliver His word, but all I've done is to enrage some people. I did not ask to be their leader, their voice. But if this was supposed to be a mission of sorts, then I failed. I could not pull them together, unite them, give them a sense of purpose. Most of them are extremely depressed, and I take blame for that. They do not understand what happened and what are they supposed to do now. And I can only talk but did not have the courage to even use my real name, or to admit I was one of them. Now it is just too late."

"I wish I had something wise to say," Grace replied softly. "But I have never heard of Him passing by Earth before. Why? I do not know. Was it for us? Or were we just inadvertent witnesses? I even thought it was for me. Maybe it's a sign from Him that I might be able to work my way to His forgiveness, at some point. Otherwise why would He leave behind something that I desperately needed? But I am sure that His motive was multi-layered and complex and all I can see with my sinful, now-human eyes is only a part of His light, and none of His reasoning. I am blind and deaf now, like you. And I am left balancing on the edge between the good and the evil, where things are gray, and distorted, and perverted."

"I have failed," Michael wailed. "I did not want this, Why was I chosen? To deepen my pain? I did not want this."

They locked eyes, understanding each other deeply. To screw it up on such a scale, to ruin a perfect thing they had both held in their palms - that takes some guts, and sparks of high intelligence, and even some humor, and intense bouts of over-confidence, and wild swings between Heaven and Hell.

"Michael, listen to me," she said. "I know what you want. I will help you reunite with your wife."

13

Chevy Chase, Maryland
Thursday

Lisa and Karen showed up together, and Walker immediately questioned the profile and the theory of a woman killer. They were both in their 70s and they were actually holding hands, terrified of being called at the police station. A blonde-haired man came from behind them and extended his hand.

"Father Matthew," he introduced himself to Mills, and gave him a hearty handshake. "I drove them here. We weren't very clear what this is all about."

Mills gestured to them to sit down on the couch in his office, and the women sat close to each other, their trembling hands neatly arranging their long skirts.

Walker and Mills exchanged a pained look.

"We are talking to everyone who saw the files of the fifty-seven people that had the alleged encounter with God,"

Mills started monotonically. "Your names came up on the list. Can you tell us how you got involved with the investigation of the phenomenon?"

"Lisa is our help in the office," Father Matthew answered quickly. "She makes copies of all documents and then stores them in the cabinets. She is doing such great work, and she invented this color-coded system so we find everything fast. We are very happy with her work. And Karen helps with Sunday school and all the kids. Sometimes she helps Lisa. That's how they saw the documents. We prepared them for the Monsignor to review."

Mills looked like he couldn't think of another question.

"Lisa, Karen," Walker said, rising from his seat with unexpected grace, "the truth is we are looking for a very bad person who appears to wish harm on these wonderful people who were touched by God."

The ladies gasped in horror.

"We were wondering if maybe you could remember if anybody else at the diocese came in contact with these documents. Maybe someone else helped you? Maybe someone looked in your color-coded cabinet when you weren't paying attention?"

"Well, we do lock up at night," Lisa explained. "And no one asked us about this."

"Frankly," Father Matthew intervened, "no one at the diocese really cares about this so-called phenomenon. We do not believe that it was God that these people saw. We prepared the report, gave it to the Monsignor, and that was that."

"I thought the Monsignor assigned an investigator?" O'Dell asked.

"Well, not really. There was some talk but the case was never opened. The Monsignor feels strongly against it."

"How can you be against something before even trying to understand it?" O'Dell sounded revolted.

"Sorry," Father Matthew said, taken aback.

"Well, I tell you what, ladies," Walker turned towards the two women. "If you remember anything at all about anybody who might have seen the documents, you will give us a call, all right?"

The women nodded, still scared. Mills opened the door. "Thanks for coming," he said. "I will show you out, but first, one minor formality - I am going to need the ladies' fingerprints."

Walker fell back in his chair, his belly button showing through an opening of his shirt. A trace of maple syrup had dripped down his jacket. O'Dell averted his eyes.

"Well," said Walker, "that's that. Where do we find the woman in New York - Grace?"

"Oh, if it's Thursday then she is at the Cathedral," answered O'Dell. "She works there from Thursday night to Sunday night, every week."

"So, is Grace a senior citizen as well?" Walker asked.

"What? Oh, no," O'Dell laughed. "She is quite young and beautiful. That's the only minor complaint we have about her, really - all the men in the church are totally smitten by her. But she never gives them a second look, never encourages them."

An intrigued Walker had some more questions, but Mills came back and interrupted them.

"Well, they do have fingers and fingerprints all right," he whined. "I wouldn't say their fingers are delicate either. We'll send the fingerprints in anyway, just in the totally off chance that they might match something at the scene. In the mean time," he brightened up, "how would you two fellows like some Korean food for lunch?"

"Ha!" Walker chuckled. "No offense but there is no better kimchi than they make on Korea Way in Manhattan."

"Bet ya," Mills said. "I know the best kimchi in Maryland. Tiny hole in the wall there in Aspen Hill. 20 minutes if we take Connecticut Ave."

"Fine, but I will be disgusted," Walker said, getting up and arranging his belt. His mouth was already salivating.

■■■

His mother used to take him out to Koreatown on Sundays after church. Walker was the youngest of the three children, and she clearly preferred him. His sisters were much older and had things to do on their own; and he was a mama's little boy, and recipient of her total and unconditional love.

His mother was a true Italian beauty back then, with long, curly dark hair and warm hazel eyes. She always wore black, as any respectable widow would do back in Sicily.

His dad had died before Walker was born, perishing from pancreatic cancer in only three months. A young man of only 40 years old, he had been kind and hard-working, and the union paid a small pension so his family could carry on. As time went on, Walker's mom transformed his memory from a good husband and father to almost that of a saint. She forgot how one night he came home smelling of wine and forgetting they had to go visit her parents; she forgot all the little faults she used to get so angry about. He attained admirable qualities just by dying, Walker thought when he was older and could see how his mom had clung to his memory as a defense against any other man who might have paid her attention.

My kids come first, she'd say when her girlfriends asked about dating this or that guy. But Walker understood that she was scared about ever having another man die on her and her kids; she couldn't have gone through that again.

He was seven years old and they would walk through Manhattan hand in hand. He remembered her hair flowing in the wind, and her black shoes clicking on the asphalt. They would pass the grocer, the Mexican guy with the flowers, the garbage bags in front of the pizza place, the cart with fresh guavas and mangoes. Then there was the fur store that was always going out of business, and then they would hit Seventh Avenue and things got bigger and cleaner. She'd stop to admire a dress in a window at Macy's, and then, giggling, they would both race to the bakery next door. She'd get an espresso, and he'd get fudge. Happiness tastes like fudge on a sunny day, watching people rush about in the big city, while Mom laughs, so close to you.

Walker finished his lunch with a sigh of satisfaction. Mills was still fighting his heaped-up plate, and O'Dell was eating some kind of plants he had long negotiated with the waiter about.

"What in the heck are those?" Walker felt like stirring the conversation.

"The only vegetarian dish they had today," O'Dell answered. "I have no idea."

"Why would you fast, exactly?" Walker wanted to know.

"To purify your body," O'Dell answered patiently, even though he could tell the question was loaded. "Plus, it's healthy for you. You…"

He wanted to say "…should try it", but Walker's killer look made him stop giving unsolicited advice.

"You know, this is like a joke setup," Walker changed course. "Two cops and a priest walk into a Korean restaurant…"

Mills laughed heartily. His phone started to ring, and as he took it out the waiter came to fill up the glasses of water. "Hold on," Mills said, and signaled Walker that he would take the call outside where it was more private.

"So what now?" O'Dell asked, finishing the last string bean.

Walker shrugged. "How about we call that Grace person?"

"Sure thing," agreed O'Dell.

Just then, Mills came back. His expression was not happy.

"Michael Dumfry?" he said hurriedly. "Dead."

"God help us," O'Dell whispered.

"Crap," Walker swore in a thick Brooklyn accent. "God damn it! We need to get ahead of this insane murderer. Why wasn't Dumfry warned? Didn't we send cops to all of these people?"

"He was warned yesterday," Mills answered wearily. "Apparently he killed himself. Also, they tell me there's a written confession. He says is the Angel of Death."

Walker squinted. . He waited for a second, and then it came - a twitch in his eye; always came when things were not exactly right.

"Can we go there?" he asked, putting his raincoat on. "I need to see this one. I am so God damn pissed right now."

14

Ocean City, Maryland
Thursday

Both Walker and O'Dell spent the first hour of the trip phoning and texting to their offices. The mood in the car was gloomy, and the rainy, gray skies didn't help.

"Michael Dumfry," Walker read aloud. "Born in Maryland. College degree, master's degree, and a Ph.D. A smart one. Married in 2007, no kids. Wife died in a car accident, he was the driver. Went to a mental hospital for a while. Hmm. Then he bought a condo in Ocean City, got a job telecommuting, rarely left home, no friends. Hmmm."

"A pretty disturbed young man," Mills commented.

"He had a tragedy in his life," O'Dell said. "How unfortunate, and I am sure he didn't fully recover. I hope that during his experience with God he found some peace."

"Oh, c'mon, you can't possibly feel any mercy for this killer," Walker interrupted him. "I hope he found no peace and he is going straight to hell where murderers belong."

"We are all children of God," O'Dell said. "If he was in such pain, he should have come and talk with us. We would have helped. I would have helped."

"Whatever," Walker mumbled.

He pulled out the nice dossier Mills had given him. He again looked at all the names, faces and profiles. After a while the noise started to clear and he began to scribble in his worn-out notebook. His tongue comically hung a little out of his open mouth; he was completely focused.

"By golly, I got it!" he finally exclaimed, swinging his notebook in the air.

"What?" asked O'Dell, looking even wearier.

"It's something you said the other night, Father. Some people heard God talk, others felt His touch, others saw things, and some heard Him breathing. Well, I categorized what everybody experienced. And look at this."

O'Dell looked at the notebook, to see a neatly designed matrix, filled out with names.

"You just drew this?" he asked in disbelief.

"I like to create crossword puzzles in my free time," Walker admitted sheepishly.

Mills, who was driving the car, turned his head toward them. "What is it?"

"Everyone who felt the breath of God is dead," Walker said in a dramatic voice. "All our victims."

They were gripped by silence.

"Well, what the hell does that mean?" Mills asked.

"I've no idea," said Walker, throwing the notebook on the seat, and he proceeded to frown again, deep in thought.

■■ ■

Walker was struck by the depressing scene. It wasn't just the old, sparse furniture and dimness of the place, but also a feeling of desperation and loneliness that he intuitively recognized. It looked like his own apartment, and Walker thought for a moment of the cops entering his residence when he was old and dead, all alone there for days; and they would have the same thoughts he was having now.

"Poor bastard," he muttered.

Michael Dumfry was lying on the couch with a syringe in his right hand. He was wearing a bathrobe and slippers. Police officers moved in and out of the room, taking pictures and dusting for fingerprints. O'Dell remained outside on the deck, in one of the large wooden chairs.

"Suicide," said Mills.

Walker nodded. "Definitely looks like it."

He huffed and puffed while taking a tour of the apartment. Why in the world they would make the hallways so narrow, he wondered. The bedroom was at the end of the corridor, in the dark. Walker opened the curtains to see another deck in the back. Nice vacation place, he thought to himself. The sheets on the bed were crumpled and not so clean, and the TV was old and chunky. Some books lay on the nightstand - *A Theory of Everything", "Daniel Martin", "One Hundred Years of Solitude", 'Warships", "The Roman Empire*", and of course, a Bible. It was dog-eared. Walker held it in his hand for a while, then shook it. No secret codes or messages fell out if it.

"We'll dust the bathroom and the bedroom good, don't you worry," Mills assured him, coming inside. "There's a glass of water in the kitchen. Some leftover mac and cheese in the fridge. Nothing else really."

Walker approached the body. It had a peaceful expression, and maybe the beginnings of a smile. Kind of hard to assume that he was murdered.

"His eyes are closed," he exclaimed. "The other poison victims had their eyes open."

"Okay," said Mills and shrugged.

"Does the door lock automatically?" asked Walker as he moved through the room.

"The door was open. The cops walked right in. Looks like he wanted to be found."

"Any blank fingerprints?"

"Nope, not yet. Only his own, and they are not burned or missing."

"No missing fingerprints, and how tall is he? What, five foot eight or so? He is not a very short man."

"Maybe he bent over when he pulled the trigger," Mills said defensively. "There are ways."

Walker huffed and puffed some more, still walking around. Finally he settled at the desk in the living room.

"Gas station receipt from Mt. Airy, the day of the murder," Mills pointed out, and Walker could have sworn he was getting almost giddy. "A Greyhound ticket to New Jersey, the day of the murder. Addresses, phone numbers, and surveillance notes on each victim. He's been planning this since almost the day it happened. Plus, of course, the big one, his last blog entry and confession that he killed them."

He sounded victorious, but Walker still had his doubts and tried to quell Mills' enthusiasm.

"Does he explain why?" Walker asked.

"Sure. Apparently he thought he was the only one who felt God's breath, and got jealous when he found out there were others. He said he wanted it all for himself, so he took the victim's last breath. However that made no difference and he felt horrible for doing it, so he decided to kill himself."

"I mean, c'mon," Walker complained, forgetting that he himself had pushed that idea earlier in the car. "How lame of a story is that. Last breath? Please. Father O'Dell! Father O'Dell!" he shouted through the door.

O'Dell stepped in, looking ghostly pale.

"Father," Walker enunciated, "what does the breath of God signify? What is it supposed to do for a person?"

"Um, if you ask from a biblical perspective, the breath of God is life. That's how Adam was created - God breathed into his lungs."

"Yeah, well..." Walker momentarily ran out of things to say.

"What is your problem?" Mills whispered, putting his arm around Walker's shoulders. "This is all lame, yes, but that's because we are dealing with religious nuts. Nevertheless, the perp confessed and he is dead. That looks like a real happy-ending to me, considering what other things this madman could have done."

"I'm sorry," said Walker. "It's just... you know, we didn't catch him. I mean, we're sitting there like idiots interrogating these poor old women, and this guy is moving in and out under our noses and taunting us like that. I am just pissed I haven't figured it out, that's all."

Mills smiled and patted his back. "It's okay," he said. "Scaring those two old ladies must have been the funniest thing that happened to me all week. Somethin' to laugh about at the dinner table tonight."

Walker's cell phone rang and he stepped onto the balcony to answer. It was the Captain.

"I guess you heard," Walker started talking immediately. "It's all over, He's completely dead now."

"Yeah, I've heard, thanks, Sieg. Good work." His voice did not sound happy though, "That's not why I called."

"Well, don't tell me there are more victims. I couldn't take it right now."

"No, no, it's not about work, Sieg. It's about your mother. She had another stroke."

Walker felt silent.

"Sieg?" the Captain continued, "She is at Mount Sinai. Come home, Sieg. They are not sure how long it will be now, and you should be here with her. I'll get Larry to wrap things up on the Angel of Death killer."

He hung up the phone and sat down on a wooden chair in the empty balcony. It was twilight already and lights started to come on along the Bay, creating rippling shadows in the water. Some people were finishing work, some were going out for dinner, others played Candyland with their kids. It was absurd and nonsensical, life. A murderer in this room; a sick beloved in the next.

His Mom's end-of-life struggle forced him to face his own mortality, and he did not like what he saw. Not everything he wanted was there; no family, no companion, no other love. It had been easier to give up after some years of dating, than to keep looking. It had been easier to just freeze inside, just keep going about work and fixing the apartment, and, after a while, reading the New York Times on a Sunday morning with his cup of coffee and bagel became such a precious routine and such a delight that he was not willing to share it with anyone anymore.

He had lived the best he could, he tried to convince himself. So he was not a great success, was not rich, and had no children to keep bearing his name; but he had put some really bad people away, and had saved several lives in his work. That was a good life, a regular life, he told himself. Then why did it feel like it was not enough; like it was all ending abruptly and fading to nothing while he powerlessly witnessed it. For the first time, things refused to be categorized in good and bad, in black and white.

He looked around himself and all he saw was hard, lonely, gray rock.

14

The Internet forgave him. The Internet had its own rules on popularity and heroism and sainthood. While Michael Dumfry was a murderer, Matt Reed was his beloved invention. He existed online and he preached online and he dictated the online culture and trends for a while; that counted for something. The Internet could not admit his failure, because it then meant that the Internet itself had failed. All the online discussions, forums, blogs, social sites and communities would then have failed.

Instead, the Internet was overwhelmed with sadness. Hundreds of thousands of words poured out. Several of the Angels of Death monikers that had appeared in the last twenty-four hours were deleted or changed.

One of the skeptics in the fifty-seven group came up with the idea: a website dedicated to Matt Reed. His blog posts were faithfully copied over to this new site, along with his several articles. His detailed biography was also posted, and many people who had known him from

before the accident that killed his wife wrote in and
added their memories. He was a regular guy, bright but
a little off, who liked to wear hats and dreamed of going
on a safari. He loved his wife, they said, and they had
dinners with friends and went to wine tastings and loved
the beach, as any other young, carefree couple.

His old friends admitted that he did not keep in touch
after the accident. He stopped talking, they heard. But
they still cared for him and wondered. They had no doubt
that Matt was touched in his divine meeting with God;
how else to explain his newly found gift of preaching?

One acquaintance, a friend of his wife, had seen him
recently; she was in Ocean City in the summer with her
kids and they were looking for a pharmacy because the
youngest one had the sniffles. As they veered off the
Boardwalk and into the quieter neighborhood on the Bay
side, she saw Michael coming out of a small apartment
building. They chatted a bit, and he seemed shy and
awkward, and answered nothing but Yes and No to her
considerate questions. And then she had to leave since
the kids had lost their patience and were pulling her by
the arms, whining. At the end of the street she turned her

head and saw him still standing there, pale, like a man who had seen a ghost.

One by one, the remaining of the fifty-seven group joined the website and posted their condolences as well. Soon, a discussion thread was created for the group only, and they could tell what they really felt without fear of being judged by others.

They all liked Matt's blog, and they were not so surprised to find he was one of them. It hadn't been easy. At first, nobody believed their story; then, in a short media frenzy, they ended up being interviewed on TV and radio, and asked crazy questions they could not answer. Then the Church stepped in and called it all a hoax, an infamy, and a blasphemy. Then reporters started to question their integrity all together, and dig up embarrassments from their lives and expose them as liars or cheaters or deranged.

But it was true. To each and every one of them, it was true. It was God who had stepped out for a walk that night, as the tip of His heel touched the Atlantic Ocean; as the kind fold of his robe swept across the East Coast.

They could not say why everyone hadn't seen it, or why the clergy, humanity's official appointees to God, were not chosen as witnesses.

There was no doubt in their minds that it had been God. Every fiber of their being had recognized Him, the original matter we were all made of. The fact that he had not left a clear message was not necessarily important. What counted was that He had come. Maybe for Him it had only seemed like a minute had passed since He created us; maybe He meant to be with us, only in His time not ours.

So one of them had snapped and killed others. They could all understand that. They had been publicly humiliated, showered with praise just because they were there, and left to wonder in their heart of hearts what it all meant. They were *all* depressed. Any one of them could have just lost it.

They kept in close contact on Matt's website. They lit virtual candles for him and wrote short verses. No one outside of the group could possibly understand how they felt, they decided. Not husbands, not children, not mothers. It had simply never happened before and a million words were not enough to describe the experience and the feelings they still had.

One of Matt's friends found an old poem Matt had written when he was just falling in love with his future wife. They replaced "heart" with "Heavens" and then it somehow fit the situation, and it somehow filled the void everyone felt.

"I am drowning in words.

The voice in the Heavens whispers thoughts

I cannot understand.

We climb through the shadows,

Up and above divine love.

Will you be silent?"

And so the Internet fell silent. The burial of Matt Reed was complete.

15

New York City

3 weeks later

Walker slept late; he opened his eyes and had the painful realization that he was totally alone. He put his glasses on and stared at the ceiling. Fresh paint, he thought. Maybe a shade of gray, with stripes. Something manly.

He made himself breakfast and wondered around in his boxers and undershirt. It was a beautiful day in Manhattan, cool and crisp, but sunny.

He had to go out, he knew. He had that gut feeling that drove him to people's doors and coffee shops where something interesting was happening. He felt his best when walking the crowded streets of Manhattan - file on the right, file on the left, wave in and out of the dense crowd. The noise of the city invigorated him and gave him ideas and clues; it was all hanging in the air like heavy fruit, to be seen and picked and enjoyed.

For absolutely no particular reason, Walker found himself walking down Madison Avenue. He stopped in front of St. Patrick's Cathedral. It was around 11:30 AM and he saw some people go inside so he followed, almost overwhelmed by the solemn entrance.

The high, arched ceiling struck him first, and he stared at it for a while, until someone else came from behind and made him move. At the right of the entrance there was a candle stand; yellow-reddish flames trembling in the slight current. He distinctly remembered what it all meant; candles were prayers, his mom used to say. Tiny specs of light in a dark universe, so God's eyes could easily find them and maybe answer them if He saw fit. There were candles for the living and candles for the dead, and some kind of rule to differentiate between the two, but Walker could not remember it exactly.

He decided to walk to the front of the church, where a handful of people were sitting   in the pews listening to a mass. He immediately recognized O'Dell, sitting at the altar, dressed up in a white robe. From the looks of it, he was just finishing the mass. He turned towards a young woman holding a baby, and made the sign of the cross in the air. They all smiled, and the young woman came down into the church and sat in a pew.

O'Dell spotted Walker right away, and waved at him happily, signaling him to wait just a minute. He tucked away his Holy Book and fussed around the altar, arranging objects that had been displaced.

"I can't believe it, Detective Walker in a church!" he laughed, finally coming down the small steps and rushing to shake his hand.

"Yeah, well…" Walker mumbled, "I was in the neighborhood, you know."

They both smiled.

"So how's everything going?" O'Dell asked warmly.

"Well, you know, my Mom passed away."

"Oh, so sorry to hear, Detective," O'Dell sighed. "How old was she?"

"Well, she was ninety-two years old. I guess she had a good, full life."

O'Dell nodded.

"We used to come here," Walker said. "When we were little, the lot of us. Every Sunday, Ma would dress us up and we would march right in. She loved this Cathedral."

"You're always welcome to come in," O'Dell said warmly. "And if you want to talk, just let me know. There is comfort in words."

Walker abstained from rolling his eyes. "Nah, thanks, I'm fine," he said. "It's all good, you know."

O'Dell looked at him intensely, as if trying to find some kind of an end of a string in there which he could pull and pull until the pain was exposed and conquered.

"Well, how are your favorite fifty-two people?" Walker asked, in an attempt to shift the focus of attention from himself.

"They're doing well," O'Dell beamed. "They actually came together for the first time as a group. Now they are meeting every week and talk with each other, and how to spread the word and how to help others. Oddly, that string of crazy murders united them and made them stronger. I am proud to say, I am running their meetings. It truly worked out miraculously."

"That's just great," Walker smiled. "A happy ending all around."

The young woman with the baby passed by them on her way out.

"Thank you for everything, Father," she said to O'Dell. "You are truly a gift from Heaven,"

"I am so glad God saw fit to help you, Grace," O'Dell said warmly. "You have a great day, and I'll see you tomorrow."

Walker caught a glimpse of her as she exited. Under her scarf, he could guess a beautiful, young face surrounded by blonde hair, She was wearing a simple blue dress and a simple coat on top. Even in the common, gray coat, she looked gracious and fetching.

"Well, I better go too," Walker said. "Really nice running into you, Father."

"Don't be a stranger," O'Dell smiled.

Walker smiled back. "Father, we both know I ain't coming back in here."

O'Dell laughed loudly.

"Oh, I missed your directness, Detective. Never say never though!"

Walker caught up with Grace in the parking lot. She was trying to open her car while juggling the baby and a large bag in her arms.

"Allow me," he said politely, and opened the car door for her. She turned to him and looked him in the eyes. Walker felt her look penetrating him, past the nice stranger image he was trying to project at the time, past the clever policeman underneath, all the way to his core - a man, sitting there as vulnerable as all men are in front of a beautiful, mysterious woman.

"Thank you," she said. She put the bag in the car, holding the baby on her left arm. Walker noticed she cringed when the baby moved in the pink blanket, like her arm hurt.

"You must be Grace," he said. "I am Detective Walker, I worked with Father O'Dell on a case."

She nodded. Her blue eyes sparkled for a second with a secret chuckle.

"How old is she?" he tried again to start a discussion. For the first time he looked at the baby, and was taken aback; the baby's face was very pale and contortioned as if it were in pain. Her blue eyes were crossed, one a bit larger than the other. A large, old scar crossed her cheek, disappearing on her tiny neck under her pink shirt. Walker needed to muster all of his strength and training to not appear shocked.

"She is nine months," Grace cooed, caressing the tiny forehead. "She looks much smaller; she was born prematurely, and very sick."

Nine months? The child could not have been heavier than 10-12 pounds.

"She is strong, I can tell," Walker said, trying his best to sound encouraging. "She will be fine."

"God will help us, right, little one?" Grace continued. "We come here every Friday when Father O'Dell has a healing mass. It's been working - she is doing better and better."

The baby moved her limp head to the right and her eyes rolled up, like she was ready to faint. Walker felt he was going to do the same. An iron claw took hold of his heart, and he felt it rip open as the little pale face turned towards him. He had never felt so much tenderness for another being.

Grace giggled softly, looking at him. "Don't be ashamed," she said. "She does this to people. She is my little angel."

She bent over gracefully and sat the girl down in her car seat.

Walker tried to regain composure. "So, do you work here at the Cathedral?" he asked, clearing his throat.

"For years, yes," Grace answered. "From Thursday to Sunday. Sometimes at the Archdiocese too." She paused deliberately: "Never missed a day."

She smiled again and Walker felt her power over him. He felt totally overwhelmed, both mentally and emotionally.

"Why only part time?" he managed to continue.

"My baby needs a lot of care," Grace said, shrugging. "I only work to make enough money for us to live on. I don't need more. I'd rather spend the time with her."

"Of course," Walker approved, not really sure of what.

He tried to find something else to say but his mind was totally blank. It felt as if everything was happening in slow motion, her lips forming words, her hair blowing in the cold breeze, her delicate hands gesturing.

"Well, it was nice meeting you, Grace," he said finally. "I hope to see you around sometime."

She smiled and made a small waving sign with her hand. Her fingers were long and white and clean, like a doll's.

Walker turned around and started walking away, when he heard her beckon. "Detective!"

He turned right around, unexpectedly happy and warm inside.

"Detective," Grace said when he approached her, "I know you lost someone close recently. Listen, you should come back to the church for a while. She is stuck out there. She needs your prayers to move on. She thinks you have not forgiven her for how she behaved when she was sick."

Her gaze was intense; she motioned him not to speak.

"No need to thank me," she whispered. "Anyone who cares for my daughter is a friend."

She got into the car and pulled away, still smiling, and Walker found himself thrown into an absolutely new world, where what Grace had said made perfect sense. Around him, waves of color, scents and possibilities became intertwined in complex patterns he had never seen before; he quietly followed the vibrating path back into the church.

16

Grace arrived at her home on Long Island in the early afternoon. She took the baby out of the car; it had fallen asleep, breathing laboriously, as if it had something stuck in its throat. The rattling breath that had kept Grace awake for weeks and weeks, dreading to see if her tiny lungs would collapse. But it had gotten much better, she told herself.

"We're home, angel," she whispered, "We're home."

The baby opened her eyes. She understood everything, Grace knew. She could tell who Mommy was, and who Grammy was. She understood colors and shapes, and showed a distinct preference for orange ever since she was born, one more reason why Grace had chosen her name to be Emmanuela. That, and because she was extraordinary and powerful in her mind, beyond mere intelligence and into the realm of the hidden truth. That, and because she was nothing but pure love.

Grace however was totally blinded; she could not tell what the child thought or felt more than any other human could. She could see people's thoughts most of the time; feel their emotions; scan and hover over a limited space if need be; but all those abilities were useless in front of her own baby.

However, their bond was undeniable. It was there as soon as Emma was born in the emergency room, with all the doctors and nurses screaming around her, trying to save them both; Grace lying there after being attacked in a dark alley, bleeding from a knife wound, feeling the baby's heart beat slowing inside of her; beyond feeling physical pain, but lost in a world of despair and decay, seeing only sharp rocks around her. Twenty-five weeks, she kept thinking. The baby is not fully grown. The baby will not live.

But there she emerged - out of all the pain and confusion, as Grace was staring at the bright white ceiling, numbed, Emma let out a survivor's little scream as she drew her first breath of air, clenching the air with her tiny hands, all 1 pound 10 ounces of her. The doctors cheered, and Grace screamed too, and cried, and as they brought Emma to her, they locked eyes as if they were one, as if they had existed together forever and now recognized each other instantly. And all of this that they call love, but a million times deeper and a million times wider struck them and bound them to each other, so that each could be made whole again.

It had been three months of sheer hell in the NICU unit at Bellevue; heart surgery, eye surgery, a myriad things going wrong every day. Grace could not even hold her daughter for the first few weeks. And through it all, Emma fought for her life with a tenacity and determination that humbled everyone who saw her.

She came home weighing three and a half pounds, with a feeding tube, and a cohort of visiting nurses. There wasn't even a room ready for her, since they had not expected the baby to arrive this soon. Grace slept with the baby in her bed, with the pager and phone at her side. The baby's raspy and guttural gasps tore into Grace's soul.

Grace opened the door to the house. It was a large Victorian house at the top of a hill, with a winding driveway lying under old oak trees. It was painted purple and blue with white-trimmed windows. From the back, the small pool peeked through the bare bushes. The house was cute and at the same time impressive. It was the house of someone who had lived there for generations, who had undeniable roots.

"Hi, Mom," she yelled as soon as she entered the hallway.

She carried Emma into the living room and set her down in her crib. She was so light - had just passed fourteen pounds a week before - and felt so fragile. Grace started to undress her, careful to not move the feeding tube on her stomach. The baby stretched, obviously happy to be out of the thick clothes.

Grace was just changing her diaper when her mom walked in. "Hello, my pretty girls," she said softly. "How was it?"

Grace turned around and gave her a quick kiss on the cheek.

"It went well," she said. "The mass was beautiful as always, Father O'Dell is just so tuned in. And then outside we met a stranger and we made friends with him. We even helped him a little."

They exchanged affectionate smiles. .

"Sorry I couldn't go this time," the older woman said. "My back is killing me today. I figured it's best if you don't have to take care of both of us in the same time."

"Don't worry about it," Grace dismissed it.

The baby was quiet now, changed and dressed up in a yellow jumpsuit with a bunny rabbit on the chest.

"How is she doing today?" the older woman whispered.

"So much better every day," Grace smiled. "Listen to her breath - it's almost normal."

"God gave her life," the older woman wept. "It is amazing, the little miracles He offers."

Grace nodded. It is I who gave Emma life, she thought. It is I who plotted to cheat Heaven and Earth, to steal God's breath of life and to tenderly give it to my sick child. It was I who figured out that the baby was slowly dying, that she would soon become another angel in the sky, while I was sentenced to never setting foot there; that we would forever be separated by an eternity.

"Just don't leave again, honey," her mom said. "A couple of weeks ago when the Archdiocese sent you to DC for a few days, she was doing so bad I thought she was going to die. And then when you came home, she immediately improved. She needs her mommy's love."

"I would do anything," Grace said. "Anything, for this child. Anything, for her to be with me for as long as I can."

"I know a mother's love. I remember the day you wandered to my door, Grace. You were only four or five years old, so lost, so adorable. I had been praying for a child for years, and there you were, all mine to keep. Never found out where you came from, or how. But I was so happy to have you."

Grace hugged her. "You gave me a great life, Mom. And now you're doing the same for her. That's all that matters."

They stood by the crib, holding each other, watching Emma sleep.

The sunlight was beginning to weaken, casting a longing ray over the floor. There was life in there, Grace thought. There was hope for a future with her daughter, even if limited by earthly laws.

I will keep bringing you His breath, my love, she promised. God's now starting to get closer to people. He's paid us a visit; there will be more, I can feel it. He is reaching out to us. There will be changes, good changes, and the human race will finally move forward in leaps and bounds. He will come again, and again I will be there, a beggar, a thief, a liar, a murderer if need be, for you, my love. For you I have defied everything, and I will do it again, and again, and again. Just so you live. Just so I can look into your beautiful eyes, and hold your tiny hand, and feel your overwhelming love. I will not think of myself or what will happen when the time comes for me; I will fully and totally sacrifice my body and soul just so you can be here, now. Breathing.

THE END